LUCKY IN LOVE

BAILEY B

Also By Bailey

Looking for some love in your life? Bailey's contemporary romances range from sweet to spicy, with everything in between.

Enemies to Lovers, High School Bully, Athlete Antihero, First Love, Girl Next Door, Completed Duet

BOOK 1 IN THE BROKEN LOVE SERIES

Piper

Most people don't think about the day they'll die. They coast through life, blissfully unaware of how their time is ticking away. I wasn't like most people. I welcomed death, wanted her to take me away from the prison I called life, but she refused. I tried twice only to survive. And then, when I thought I had nothing left it came.A reason to live.Rex was a small, unexpected ray of light my world of darkness that blossomed into a beam of sunshine. I thought, maybe this was why Death didn't take me. Maybe she knew that if I held on a little longer things would turn around. But the third time Death came to my door wasn't by choice. Someone else brought her, and I fear this time she might take me.

Rex

Being the son of a country star sucks. My parents are never around, I move every year or so, and I have no real friends. Everyone around me has an agenda. Everyone except Piper Lovelace. I can't get that girl to notice me. Trust me I've tried.Thankfully, fate stepped in and gave me the break I needed. I've got her attention, now I need her to give me a chance.

Enemies to Lovers, High School Bully, Athlete Antihero, First Love, Girl Next Door, Completed Duet

BOOK 2 IN THE BROKEN LOVE SERIES

She's beautiful. Fierce. Nothing at all like the girl I used to know, which is absolutely terrifying because Danika Winters is the only person outside of that room who knows the truth. She could ruin me, and I'm not talking about my reputation. I couldn't give two shits about what the kids at St. A's think. I'm talking major, life-altering, jail time ruined. I'll do whatever it takes to keep her quiet. Even if it means destroying the only person I've ever cared about.

Asher Anderson is a dick.

We aren't friends, so when he seeks me out in the cafeteria on the worst day of my life, I'm suspicious. When he tells Liam Heiter that we're dating, which couldn't be farther from the truth, I want to kill him...Until I see Liam's reaction.

Liam—my best friend, the guy who crushed every hope of us *officially* being together—is jealous. He has never looked at me this way and I love it.

So, I play along. Maybe watching me with someone else will make Liam suffer like I have the past four years. And maybe, just maybe, he'll come to his senses and realize we belong together. It's not like I actually *like* Asher. At best, I tolerate him. What's the worst that can happen?

**Fall In love with a
Bailey Black Book Here**

Small town, Opposites attract, Cowboy, New girl in town,
Unexpected parenthood (+denial)

Josh

I met the girl of my dreams in a church parking lot while my best friend was having sex in my truck. Her name was Layla and she was trying her hardest to ignore me and them from two parking spaces over. I swear, I've never seen someone so beautiful in my life. I've also never struggled to get the girl but,for some reason, my foot and my mouth became friends that night in the worst of ways.

Cheesy pickup line, that failed? Check.
Inability to form coherent sentences? Check.
Ego crushing letdown? Yup. That happened, too.

I can't put my finger on it, but there's something about Layla that sucks me in. I need to get to know her. Spend time with her. Make her mine. Who knows, maybe she will be the one to finally settle me down. That is, if I can convince her to give me the time of day.

Layla

Everything about Joshua Thomas screams, run away. His sharp jaw. Those vibrant eyes. Lush lips that have probably tasted every girl in this tiny town. I know better than to give him a chance, but knowing what I should do and listening are two different things. He makes my heart flutter in ways I thought only possible in Hallmark movies. He makes my legs shake from one look. I resisted him once. I don't know if I can do it again.

Second chance, The dare/bet, Insta chemistry, Learning to love, Shared Pasts

I've sworn off men forever! Okay, not forever, but for a few months. After my last hook-up, my vag needs a reset because the last man to touch me broke it in the worst of ways. Not a problem until my new dance partner comes into the picture. He's turning into my forbidden fruit, tempting me in ways I didn't know possible.

I have three months of celibacy ahead of me and eight weeks to whip my new dance partner into shape.

Someone save me.

Scan to Read a Sample

Fake dating, Second chance, Friends to lovers, Everybody can see it, Short and Spicy novella

A wedding. A lie. And regret.

I'm in over my head with not one but two ex-boyfriends at the same wedding. Both of which I haven't seen in over a year. When the one who ripped my heart into pieces backs me into a corner, I grab the other and kiss him.

Yup. This is how I ended up fake dating Noah Ruckers, and let me tell you, it's an emotional roller coaster. I thought I'd put my feelings for him behind me. We spent years as friends after our break up, nothing more. But no matter how hard I try I can't forget what his lips feel like. Or the way his arms wrap around me.

In two days, I'm walking away. There is no future for us. But that doesn't mean I can't pretend.

Fall In love with a
Bailey Black Book Here

Fake dating, Second chance, Friends to lovers, Everybody can see it, Short and Spicy novella

Holly Flynn is a leprechaun who grants wishes—but with a dangerous twist. Each wish comes at a price: once it's fulfilled, the "victim" forgets everything before their wish—and her.

When a gorgeous stranger asks for one unforgettable night, things take an unexpected twist. The chemistry between them is electric, and soon, Holly's struck by a terrifying thought: She doesn't want him to forget her.

Then, a week later, he knocks on her door. And he remembers everything.

Why does he remember, when no one else does? Is it fate—or is her magic betraying her?

**Fall In love with a
Bailey Black Book Here**

How About a Fantasy Adventure?

Dive into the completed Neverland Novels. Characters have been aged up for this darker, grittier version. If you like your fairytale retellings with hot, ruthless, morally gray love interests, you'll enjoy this series. The Lost Darling is the first book in the main storyline. Please read this series in order.

Twisted Fairy Tale, Peter Pan Retelling, Multiple Love Interests, Morally Gray Males, She's Mine, Scorching hot lost boys, Spice, and more!

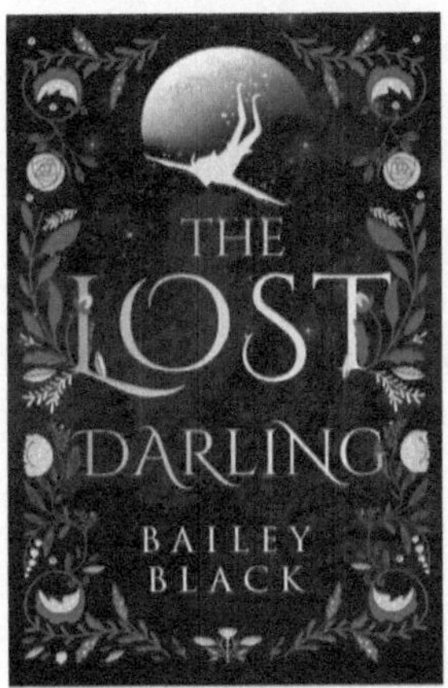

Second star to the left and continue until morning.

I got that line tattooed on my wrist the day I turned twenty-one. So much symbolism in such a simple sentence. At the time, it was a nod to the future and the infinite possibilities to come, while reminding me to remember the past and to look for magic in the world.

Growing up, nothing was ever what it seemed. The shift of leaves on a tree was a faery skipping by. Shooting stars were a chance to make wishes. Shadows were souls stuck between this world and the next, mirroring a life they once had.

My imagination was limitless, the world a wonderful adventure waiting to unfold.

It's easy to lose that sense of wonder with the weight of life on your shoulders and I wanted a reminder to get me through the hard days.

Most importantly, it was an ode to the boy who earned the title of my first crush, even if he was animated. Peter Pan wasn't a *save the damsel* kind of prince. He was daring, and selfless, and took care of the ones he loved. He was a friend to all but never afraid to fight the Pirates when their moral compass broke. Wendy was an idiot for leaving him. She rushed home to a heartless world full of men willing to lie through their teeth to get down her pants.

But that's the beauty of a book, the characters are perfectly flawed. Damaged just enough that we still love them. Whereas reality is nothing but empty promises and baggage the size of mountains.

The day I got my tattoo, I would have given anything to be whisked away into a fairytale. My world was crumbling, and all I wanted was to go back to when life was simpler. I didn't realize I had sealed my fate in ink.

Branded myself as one of the Lost.

Neverland was everything the stories made it out to be. Beautiful. Full of magic. Filled with handsome men and debonair pirates. But the author of my favorite tale left out one crucial detail.

In order to get there, you have to die.

A witch in a world where magic is illegal, A revenge mission, A rescue mission, Death. People die. Sorry, not sorry, 2 love interests (not a RH and not a triangle), A touch of enemies to lovers. He falls first she falls harder

I had a plan. Find the soldier who killed my family and make him pay. It should have been an easy feat. I'd done it over a dozen times, taking out each member of that regiment one by one, but the mission went sideways. It all started with the man in the woods. The one my webs of magic couldn't sense even when he stood before me. Then my partner made a mistake, and now he's lying in one of the Crown's dungeons, fighting for his life. I couldn't leave him to die, but I couldn't just walk into the castle either.

Or maybe I could.

With the help of some unexpected allies, I entered the Culling—a one-in-a-lifetime chance to become queen. I have no interest in winning the prince's heart, or the crown. My only goal is to get into the castle, find my friend, and get out before someone realizes I'm a Cerise.

But when the welcome ball turns from a grand event into a nightmarish dance of death, all eyes are on me. As if that's not bad enough, the soldier, the one who took my family, he's here.

If you loved "The Selection" by Kiera Cass and "From Blood and Ash" by Jennifer L. Armentrout, get ready to fall in love with this enchanting fantasy romance!

**Fall In love with a
Bailey Black Book Here**

Chapter 1

HOLLY

"Wanna get lucky?" a deep voice asked, barely audible over the clamor of music and conversations vibrating throughout O'Malley's Pub.

I recognized the phrase and smiled brightly at a blonde man with thick-rimmed glasses who'd just unknowingly entered himself into a game of luck by reading the gold letters sprawled across my chest.

"I'm a leprechaun." I grinned and spun around to lift my long brown hair, revealing the echoing phrase printed on the back of my green shirt.

The man chuckled and raised his beer to his lips, hazel eyes flicking back to the letters on my chest. This time, though, I knew he wasn't reading them. His gaze lingered, holding a fraction of a second too long to be innocent. Usually, I'd find such blatant ogling irritating, but tonight, the brazenness worked in his favor. This was exactly the kind of man I was looking for—gullible and predictable.

"Are you now?" he asked, his grin widening into a cocky smile that probably landed him more than a few phone numbers on a good night. He extended his hand. "I'm Ryan."

I gave a soft, noncommittal hum and shook it. His palm and fingers were soft, and I couldn't help but wonder what he did for a living. Computer scientist? Massage therapist? Gynecologist? It didn't matter. I wouldn't see Ryan past tonight, so I brushed the thought away.

I had one goal for him and one goal only. "Want to play a game, Ryan? Leprechauns love games."

"Do they?"

I nodded, flashing a bright, flirtatious smile of my own.

"Ok. I'll play your game, but let's get a table first." He reached for my hand and I felt nothing, just the lingering chill of his mug. No spark of attraction or even a warm hum of curiosity. It was like my heart knew that no matter how handsome, and Ryan was classically handsome, there was no place for love on a night like tonight.

What I did notice, though, was the prickling sensation of my magic stirring under my skin, eager to play with its next victim.

Ryan chose a recently vacated table in a quiet-ish corner and casually set his half-empty mug down as if this was a normal part of life. Him flirting with a girl. Me—said girl—doe eyed and smiling, falling into every one of his practiced charms.

He leaned in, positioning himself as close as possible without us actually touching. It was a calculated move. One I appreciated. I liked that Ryan was interested but not pushy. If tonight were any other night, I might've struck up a conversation and given him a fair shot despite my first impression.

But I wasn't looking for a hookup.

My magic only worked one night a year—March seventeenth, St. Patrick's Day—and I needed to play as many games as possible.

"Tell me a secret," I said, my voice hovering just above a whisper. "And I might grant you a wish."

"What kind of secret?"

"That's up to you." I leaned closer until our arms touched. Heat radiated off Ryan in uncomfortable waves. I wanted to retreat to the patio where the crisp Nocatee air would cool me off.

Unfortunately, this trap was already set and the clock was

ticking. My magic wouldn't let me walk away until Ryan either refused the offer, I rejected the secret, or the deal was complete.

Meaning I was stuck.

"But the darker, the more twisted your secret, the better your odds are of having your wish granted."

Ryan rubbed his chin, brushing his fingers over the short, uneven stubble. I could practically see the gears in his brain spinning. I'd easily bet a hundred dollars that he assumed my game was some form of roleplay gimmick, and he probably thought playing along would bring him one step closer to getting laid.

That look, the one confirming every stinking one of my suspicions, told me I was right. Ryan was, in the most basic of ways, just like every other participant in my game.

I tried to remember the last time someone took me by surprise and made the game fun. It had been a long time. The first few years of tapping into my magic were the best. I enjoyed the rush of finding people to play with and seeing my magic change lives. Granted, the things people wished for were usually superficial, but I loved it nonetheless.

That was almost ten years ago. Now, my magic felt more like a burden than a blessing. The secrets I harvested a tithe to be paid each year or else...

Truthfully, I didn't know what would happen if I didn't use my magic. It could wither away. It could eat away at me, literally taking my soul and strength until I was a tattered shell of myself and eventually died. Not using it could summon my father, which would be worse than actually dying. Or I could be sucked into the Otherworld, forced to be a slave to an unruly creature as penance for my disobedience. Mother was clear in relaying the warnings when my magic matured.

And she was just as clear with the loophole.

I was half-human. If the day ever came that I found my soul-mate and fell in love, I could leave my lineage behind and live a normal life. I used to think the idea of being like everyone else, being truly human, was a fate worse than death. Now, I found myself considering it more nights than not.

"You know, I've always wanted a Viking beard. Can your magic grant me that?" Ryan's tone was playful and teasing. He didn't believe I could grant his wish. I tilted my head, pretending to think about my answer. This was the cat-and-mouse part of the game, the only part I still found to be fun.

"Maybe," I replied, trying my best to sound mysterious. "It depends on your secret. What's something no one knows?"

Ryan leaned closer, the tips of his ears reddening as he dropped his voice. "I still sleep with a teddy bear named Mr. Fluffypants, and I'm thirty-two."

I bit my lip to stifle a laugh. I tried to imagine what that must look like and couldn't help but picture Ryan in an adult-sized onesie, sleeping with his thumb in his mouth. It was impossible not to smile at the sight, but I cleared my throat and forced myself to sound serious. "Scandalous."

"Embarrassing is more like it," Ryan muttered, finishing his beer. The flush on his cheeks faded as his confidence returned. "So, now that I've kept my end of the deal, can you keep yours? Or should we find a different currency to exchange?"

My laugh slipped out before I could stop it. I had zero interest in a threesome with this man and Mr. Fluffypants, but his secret was undeniably amusing. I would grant his wish.

I breathed in Ryan's words, letting them wrap around the strand that tethered me to my lineage. Warmth pooled in my center as the magic spread. It built inside me, slow at first and then overwhelmingly fast until it released in a hot rush that was almost orgasmic. In mere seconds, a long, coarse beard emerged from Ryan's chin, the thick strands spreading across his face and down to his chest.

"It was nice meeting you," I said, dismissing him as I turned to leave.

Ryan didn't argue or even try to convince me to stay. He'd already forgotten who I was. That was the beauty of my magic.

My victims didn't remember their world being different before the wish, if I granted it, or me.

I turned quickly, high on the lingering energy, but barely made it five steps before bumping into a hard body. I jumped instinctively, and nearly fell backward, but was quickly wrapped in the arms of a stranger as the smell of cedar and spice swirled through my senses.

"Sorry," I muttered, looking into the eyes the color of Montana Sapphires.

The stranger's lips lifted into a pearly white smile, and I was stunned.

Mesmerized.

The man wasn't wearing a lavish St. Patrick's Day outfit like most of the people in the bar were. No *Kiss Me I'm Irish* shirt or a speck of green. Nor was he shirtless and in a kilt like some of the other men in the room, although the strange thought that I'd love to see him like that floated into my mind. Despite not being dressed for the holiday, he looked effortlessly handsome in blue jeans fitted with a long-sleeved button-down shirt with the top button undone.

And... familiar.

"I'm not sorry," he said, his voice as smooth as velvet.

Something stirred inside me, a pull stronger than anything I'd felt before. I took a step back, instinctively wary. I'd had crushes before and felt sparks of attraction, but this was different.

I glanced around, looking for my sister, Dahlia—a heart weaver. A gentry with the ability to feel and enhance people's emotions. Some people might call her a cupid. She loved playing matchmaker, though her gift, unlike mine, wasn't restricted to one day a year. If Dahlia sensed strong enough emotions, she would give people the push they needed to make a move.

I'd never felt Dahlia's power before, but right now, I wondered if my sister was up to something because this pull tasted like magic.

And if it wasn't Dahlia meddling, then what kind of trouble was I about to get myself into?

Chapter 2

LIAM

I twisted a mug of frothy, green beer against the sticky high-top table, my fingers absently tracing condensation that slid down the glass. The noise around me was over-whelming —laughter, clinking mugs, and the occasional cheer from a group glued to the TVs overhead. The chaos didn't help my mood.

I was tired.

Exhausted.

Three months into a bet with my brothers and I was no closer to finding someone to marry. If I couldn't find someone, let alone make them fall in love with me by the end of the summer, I'd lose everything. Well, not everything, but the only thing that mattered.

I twisted the mug again, remembering how I thought winning would be easy. The rules were simple: find a pretty girl. Wine, dine, and woo her. Lock her in with a ring, and then *bam!*

But it hadn't been that easy. Every girl I'd met hadn't been right. There was something about each Tinder date and bar hookup that left me unsatisfied. Longing. Sounding like a fucking pussy.

A small, potentially psychotic, part of me was relieved. I'd never admit it out loud, but I didn't want the pressure of running the family empire. Six restaurants and three bars were overwhelming. I was happy with my slice of heaven, Abbott's, and if it wasn't tangled up in the web of the bet I wouldn't even be trying.

I spun the mug once more, grimacing as I caught a faint whiff of the crap this bar tried to pass as beer. It had a faintly metallic taste like it had been brewed in a tin can. It was probably the worst drink I'd had in months.

I sighed and stared at the two inches of foam on top of the green liquid. Tonight was supposed to be a break, one night away from the weight of the bet. No scouting. No wondering if this girl or that could be the one. Just one drink, definitely not this one, and maybe a conversation or two.

But even that seemed impossible. Instead, I'd spent the last fifteen minutes spiraling deeper into my thoughts, the idea of being a silent partner as a forty percent shareholder of the bar I built from the ground up gnawing at me.

"Maybe I should've stayed home," I muttered, closing my eyes. My couch and a quiet movie night sounded like heaven right now. Hell, even going to bed before midnight felt like a better choice than sitting here drowning in self-pity and bad beer.

When I opened my eyes, a woman in a shiny green dress stood on the other side of my table. "You're quite curious, you know that?" she said, her voice carrying a lilting tone of mischief. "I can figure out what everyone desires in this room, except you."

I blinked, caught off guard because...what? The woman made no sense. She had to be drunk; it was the only rational explanation. I waited for her to smile, laugh, or give me some noticeable indication she was joking, but she just stared at me.

"Maybe that's because you don't know me," I replied, my tone sharper than intended.

She didn't seem to notice. Instead, she grinned and extended a delicate hand. "I don't have to know someone to know what their hearts want but, if it helps, I'm Dahlia."

Her hand was small and cool against mine as I shook it. I took her in, trying, despite swearing that I'd take the night off, to determine if she could be *the one*.

She had burgundy red hair that tumbled over her shoulders in long, straight strands, a smattering of freckles across fair skin, and green eyes more vibrant than the drink in her hand. She was pretty and outgoing, and I had no reason to cross her off my list of potentials. Except she didn't *feel* like the one.

"And you are?" Dahlia prompted when I didn't respond.

"Liam."

"Ah, Irish for 'strong-willed warrior.' Are you Irish?"

"Not that I'm aware of," I quipped, but I'd been called a less friendly version of strong-willed on more than one occasion. Nature of the beast when you own a bar and frequently play bouncer to kick assholes out. Or when you have three older brothers who'd never looked at you like you were worth a damn. I'd done many foolish things simply because I was too stubborn to lose whatever had been wagered.

Hence my current predicament.

"Hmm, pity. That would make more sense." Dahlia sighed dramatically, taking a slow sip of her fizzy green drink through a black paper straw. "I can't get a read on you and it's driving me mad."

I raised an eyebrow, curious despite knowing I should disengage and leave. "Because you can tell everyone's desires?"

"Yup." She popped the "p" with exaggerated flair. "It's my blessing and my curse."

"Prove it."

Dahlia's grin widened at the challenge and she leaned back, casually scanning the room. After a quiet moment, she pointed at the man across the bar with her straw. "Sex," she said and then pointed to the next person and then the next. "Sex. Cookies. Sex. To leave. A nap. Sex."

Despite myself, I snorted. This was crazy and yet I was sucked in, unable to walk away.

"What about her?" I nodded toward the brunette at the far corner of the bar chatting with a blonde man in thick-rimmed glasses.

To Holly Flynn.

I noticed her twice tonight, and both times, she was talking with someone new. I couldn't tell if she sought the men out or if they were as drawn to her as I was, but unlike them, I wasn't in the mood to get shot down. If I added her to the lot of women who couldn't be the one for some reason or another, that would make her number... I didn't even know. I didn't want to know.

Dahlia followed my gaze and when she found the brunette, her lips curved knowingly. "Oh, interesting," she murmured more to herself than to me. "That one? She wants to have fun."

"What kind of fun?" I asked, watching as she laughed at something the blonde man said. The sound carried like music over the chatter of the bar and it struck a nerve inside me.

It pissed me off.

I was angry—jealous even—which was stupid because we hadn't spoken in years, not since college. Not since I blew my chance with her.

"The kind where she gets to play games without worrying about strings."

"She's not going to find that here," I said, frowning, unable to tear my gaze away from her.

She was magnetic.

Beautiful in a subtle kind of way that slapped you in the face. Holly wasn't in an over-the-top, sexy outfit like most of the women out tonight. Just jeans and a white T-shirt with gold letters. If she wore makeup, it was subtle—natural looking. Long brown hair fell in loose waves to the middle of her back, but she twisted one strand through her fingers. *Was she nervous or flirting?*

"Maybe. Maybe not." Dahlia leaned in conspiratorially. "Perhaps you could help her."

Unlikely. Glasses-guy was giving Holly bedroom eyes and she...

She leaned closer to him. Her arm brushed against his and I was no expert, but I was pretty sure that meant she was into him. "She seems happy enough with that guy."

"Ugh," Dahlia groaned dramatically. "Trust me, that won't last more than five minutes. But you two... You could be great—if you know the rules."

I tore my gaze away from Holly to fix Dahlia with a skeptical look. "What are you talking about?"

"She's playing a game," Dahlia said pointedly. She waited for me to put the pieces she'd laid out together, but they made no sense. When I didn't respond, she added, "Tell her a secret, and she'll grant you a wish. That man is almost to the end of his game, but you could outsmart her. Wish to spend the night together—no sex, no tricks. Just a night of fun."

Her game. Right. I was surprised Holly was still doing that after all these years. Then again, back in college, she always said this was her favorite holiday. I had the chance to play once and blew it. Holly rejected my wish for a date, before even hearing my secret. "And why would she agree to that? She doesn't know me."

Dahlia's grin widened. "Because I know my sister. Holly won't be able to resist."

"Sister?" I said, frowning, the single word enough to pull me away from the temptation of crossing the bar. My gaze flicked from Holly to Dahlia and then back again. "You two look nothing alike."

"Half-sister, but that's not important," Dahlia said, her tone turning serious for the first time. "Trust me, she'll love you."

I shook my head, smirking faintly. Now, things were making sense. Dahlia was playing matchmaker. It was flattering, if not a little odd. If only she knew I'd already tried once, during freshman year, and struck out. "And here I thought you were trying to hook up with me." I touched my chest and pretended to be sad. "I'm heartbroken."

"You'll be heartbroken if you don't act fast." Dahlia plucked the mug of warm beer from my hand and shoved me forward. "Now, go!"

Chapter 3

O'Malley's buzzed with life—the clink of glasses, bursts of raucous laughter, and the hum of a hundred conversations merging into a single, chaotic melody. Yet, somehow, it all faded into the background when this man touched me. It was just him and me, standing there in the thick haze of fryer grease and stale beer.

My pulse thundered in my ears as his hand closed over mine, warm and steady, like it belonged there. I stepped closer to the high-top table behind me, and the sticky floor tugged at my heels. It grounded me in a way my spiraling thoughts couldn't. I glanced up at him, catching the way the dim, flickering neon lights played off his green eyes.

This had to be Dahlia's doing. My sister loved meddling and this situation screamed of her handiwork. But why tonight? Why him?

I wanted to look around, to search the room for her telltale smirk, but I couldn't tear my gaze from *him*. A flash of heat surged through me. His presence was thrilling, almost intoxicating.

And terrifying.

So, so terrifying.

"I really should go," I said, the words weak and unconvincing, even to my own ears.

"Wait!" he said quickly, his voice low but insistent. His grip on my hand didn't tighten, but it was firm enough to keep me rooted. His eyes locked onto mine, and for a moment, I thought I saw something vulnerable flicker there.

"I promised my brothers I'd find a wife before the end of summer," he said, his tone calm but tinged with something darker. "If I don't, I lose the only thing I've ever cared about."

I blinked, startled. "Why are you telling me this?"

My voice barely rose above the background noise, but it didn't matter. His words had already triggered the familiar stir of my magic. It coiled in my chest, threading through my veins like a living thing. My breath caught at the realization that the binding was happening—my power responded to his confession, wrapped itself around his words, and tethered me to his secret before I'd even heard his wish.

No! My thoughts raced, trying to understand what was happening. My magic had never betrayed me before—never acted of its own accord. It always obeyed me, like an extension of my will. But tonight, the rules we'd followed for years had somehow changed.

He smiled faintly with a practiced sort of ease that didn't reach his eyes. "Those are still the rules, aren't they? I tell you a secret, and you grant me a wish. That's how this works."

I forced a laugh, though panic simmered beneath the surface. "Let me guess—you wish for me to be your wife?"

His laugh was genuine this time, a soft, rich sound that caught me off guard because I'd heard it before. I just couldn't remember where. "You're beautiful, but no. That'd be weird and it would break the rules."

"Then what do you want?"

"To spend the night with you," he said simply, as if it were the most natural thing in the world.

"Oh!" I said, stunned again. This was a first. I was used to people wishing for money, cars, or bigger body parts—frivolous, superficial things.

Never for me.

I suddenly felt anxious. I was bound to this man, for better or worse, for the rest of this night, and he wanted *me*. I flagged down a passing waitress because I would need a drink to get through this wish...or five.

"A frothy green glass of whatever your special is tonight," I said.

The waitress nodded, sparing my new partner a glance, but he shook his head politely.

I crossed my arms and leaned against the table's edge, letting my gaze settle on him. He looked casual enough, lounging back in his chair, but the faint crease at the corner of his mouth gave him away. He wasn't as at ease as he pretended to be. His wish had him rattled. Hell, it had me rattled! How did he even know the rules?

I'd never had someone eavesdrop on me before, even when others were standing directly next to my victim. As soon as I asked if they wanted to play a game, a magical barrier went up that kept outsiders from hearing our conversation. So, how did he hear, and why didn't I notice him listening?

Not that it mattered.

He wasn't going anywhere. The binding my magic used on us ensured that. What he didn't know—what he didn't need to know—was that the spell had already set in place. I might not be able to leave his side, but I could use this ignorance to my advantage and do some digging. "Two questions before I decide whether to grant your wish."

"Ask away."

"First," I said, arching a brow, "what's your name?"

"Liam," he replied, his tone carrying a hint of arrogance, as though I should already know. That irked me because I felt like I should know it. He felt so familiar, like a dream I'd wandered into for a second time. I just couldn't figure out why.

"Holly." I gave a slight nod, watching him carefully as I introduced myself. My name didn't phase him. There was no microexpression of its processing. *Curious. Too, too curious.* "Next question —tell me about the rules of your bet."

"Oh, nothing groundbreaking," Liam said, running a hand through his tousled dark hair. "The usual bargain nonsense. If I don't convince someone to marry me by the end of the summer, I lose thirty percent of the family business and sixty percent of the place I built from scratch. They wanted to hit me where it hurt. You know, typical sibling rivalry stuff."

I blinked. Typical sibling rivalry? What kind of family did this guy come from? "Shouldn't you be out searching for a wife then? You know, instead of hanging around with me tonight."

"Probably," he admitted with a deep exhale, his shoulders sagging slightly. "But I wanted one night—one night without the pressure of wondering if she's *the one*."

"Sounds tiresome." I let my voice dip into something that sounded like sympathy, though it wasn't. Or shouldn't have been. Liam was like every other mark. Our time together was limited. What happened beyond tonight *couldn't* matter because even if I wanted to help, I wouldn't be able to.

"You have no idea," he said, a bitter edge creeping into his tone. "Which is why I'm looking forward to tonight. Just one normal night."

I tapped my fingers against the table, feigning thoughtfulness. Tonight would be anything but normal, but who was I to burst his bubble? "Well, I should probably inform you of one of mine. Let you know we only have two hours together."

"What?"

"You asked to spend the night with me, right?" I said, leaning in slightly. "Well, the night ends at midnight. At 12:01, your wish will have been fulfilled." My grin widened. "You've got to be specific when bargaining with the fae folk."

Liam glanced at the gold letters printed on my shirt and smirked. "Because you're a leprechaun?"

"Precisely." I winked just as the waitress arrived with my

drink—a frothy, neon-green concoction that practically screamed *drink me and you'll be puking later*.

Before I could stop him, Liam handed the waitress a five-dollar bill, brushing off my protest with an easy smile.

"Thanks," I said, raising the glass to my lips. I took a small, tentative sip, only to fight back a grimace. It was bitter and hoppy, with an aftertaste like burnt grass. "Delicious," I lied, setting the mug down quickly.

"That bad, huh?" he asked, laughing.

"Terrible," I admitted, pushing the drink aside. "I owe you five dollars for that."

"Don't worry about it," Liam said, standing and offering his hand. "There's somewhere I want to take you."

I eyed his outstretched hand warily. I couldn't refuse. If I did, the pain would start as an uncomfortable tingle and mount into excruciating pain. But there were no stipulations about me delaying the inevitable and setting some ground rules. "Just so we're clear, sex is off the table. If you're thinking of taking me back to your place, you might as well save yourself the time and energy."

"If I had a heart, it'd be breaking right now," he said, pouting dramatically.

"Heartless, huh?"

"So says my ex-girlfriend," Liam said softly, his voice taking on an almost reflective tone. "Makes finding a soulmate pretty difficult, don't you think?"

I froze mid-step, his words sending a ripple of unease through me. Was it what he said or how he said it? Before I could press him further, Liam took my hand and gave it a gentle tug, urging me to follow.

"Our time is ticking," Liam said with an easy smile that didn't quite reach his eyes. "Let's make the most of it."

Chapter 4

The streets buzzed with a strange energy as Liam and I walked side by side, a blend of chaos and quiet. On one side, the shops stood closed and dark, their windows lifeless against the night. But on the other, bars came alive, pulsing with music and neon lights. Every so often, laughter or a drunken shout would cut through the rhythmic thumping bass that echoed through the night.

I glanced at Liam, letting a smirk play on my lips. Walking next to him was easy. There was no pressure to make conversation or awkwardness lingering in the quiet. There was just a tingle in my center and a feeling of familiarity. Something I couldn't quite pin but wanted to discover. "You're not one of those creeps who's going to murder me, are you? Just so you know, I'm fully not murderable."

Liam's brows shot up, and a laugh escaped him, warm and genuine. "Not-murderable? What does that even mean?"

"It means you wouldn't want to kill me," I explained, waving a hand dramatically. Out of the blue, I was nervous—not scared—but my heart raced again, and I felt a little anxious at the thought of explaining why I was special. I mean why I'd be missed. "Well, for starters, people would notice. I have three sisters who are constantly up my butt. They'd sound the alarm if I went MIA for more than twenty-four hours. Plus, I've got a cat, two guinea pigs, and a succulent garden.

Deny them their care, and you'll have bigger problems than me."

Liam's head tilted as he shook it, his lips tugging into a reluctant smile. "Noted. Lucky for you, I'm not the murderous type."

"Isn't that exactly what a murderer would say?" I teased, stepping closer so my shoulder brushed against his. A zing of warmth shot through me. I eased away, unsure what to make of the feeling. Was it magic? Or something more...

"So, where are you taking me, Mr. Not-a-Murderer?"

Liam gestured ahead, his gaze steadily still on me. "Have you ever been to Abbott's?"

"Of course I have. It's the most popular spot in the city, but there's no way we're getting in. Tonight is a special event night. Unless you have pre-ordered tickets, which I doubt considering the shithole we just left, we'll be stuck in line all night with like zero chance of getting in."

Liam tucked his hands into his pockets and shrugged. The action was so inconsequential, so mundane, but there was something in the way he looked at me. I couldn't explain it, but it felt like he had a secret.

"I did *not* pre-order tickets. I actually planned to stay as far away from that place as possible, but something tells me you could go for a drink that doesn't taste like ass and maybe a little fun."

"You're not wrong," I admitted, folding my arms. "But unless you've got some serious connections..."

"You don't know half of what I've got," he interrupted smoothly. "You don't know me yet."

I snorted. "Touché. Speaking of things I don't know, what's your last name?"

His confidence faltered, just for a second, but then it was back in place, like a mask protecting him from the outside world. "I think I'd rather not say."

"Secrets. Secrets." I teased, nudging him lightly. "Fine, I'll start. Mine is Flynn. See? Easy. Now, it's your turn."

"Smith," he replied too quickly.

"Smith," I whispered, rolling it over my tongue. I couldn't explain it, but the name didn't *feel* right. I felt crazy, but my intuition had never steered me wrong. His last name was definitely not Smith. I stopped mid-step, narrowing my eyes. "Really?"

"Yeah. Problem?" Liam said, his expression unreadable.

Yes. I pretended to think it over and then shrugged. I was in no place to judge Liam. I'd kept the secret of what my family was all my life. He probably had a reason not to tell me who he was, so I decided not to push the matter. "It's fine, I guess. Pretty basic, though. I expected something cool like Pitt or Coleson."

Liam looked up at the sky and chuckled. "Good thing my name isn't all I've got going for me."

As we turned the corner, the line outside Abbott's came into view, snaking down the block with impatient chatter and bursts of laughter. My stomach sank looking at it. I'd only been to Abbott's twice and both experiences were amazing. Tonight would probably be just as fun.

If we could get in.

"You only have two hours left of your wish. Actually," I pulled my phone from my back pocket and glanced at the screen. "A little less. Are you sure you want to waste it standing in line?"

Liam didn't slow down. "I can spend my time however I want."

"With some restrictions," I shot back, mostly as a reminder to myself.

"Exactly." Liam reached for my hand, his fingers brushing mine before locking them together. My breath hitched as a jolt of heat shot through me. I stared at our joined hands, unsure of what to make of the butterflies suddenly swarming in my chest.

A terrifying thought flickered through my mind so fast it left with a shudder.

Am I...

Could he be...

Is this why Dahlia messed with my love life *tonight*?

No. I shook my head, refusing to consider the idea and followed quietly. We walked past the line, ignoring the irritated glances and muttered complaints. A burly man stood at the door with arms crossed, his skeptical gaze shifting when he saw us. I swallowed hard and prepared myself for the mortification of being turned away at the door. There was no doubt in my mind that the people we passed were staring, waiting to laugh at us when we made the walk of shame to the back of the line.

"Ralph," Liam greeted, his voice carrying an easy confidence as he nodded at the bouncer.

The bouncer's broad face twisted from confusion to shock. "What are you doing here?" Then, as if catching himself, he blurted, "Not that you shouldn't be here. I mean, you can be here, obviously. Just... it's unexpected."

Liam arched a brow, the corner of his mouth twitching to fight another one of those disarming smiles. "Relax, Ralph. It's fine. I just wanted to show this pretty girl a good time. Is that alright with you?"

Ralph's eyes darted to me, briefly taking me in before returning to Liam. "Does she know about the... you know?" he asked, his voice dropping conspiratorially.

Liam sighed a long-suffering sound. "Dude. Really?"

"Right. Sorry." Ralph straightened, stepping aside quickly as if to make up for the slip. "Are we still on for Tuesday?"

"I wouldn't miss it," Liam replied, guiding me inside with a light hand on my back.

As we stepped into Abbott's, the familiar sound of *DropKick Murthy's* filled the air, weaving through the hum of conversation and the clinking of glasses. I glanced around the room, taking in the warm glow of hanging lights and the polished wood that gave the place a rustic, cozy charm. Green shamrocks and streamers were everywhere. It looked as if Party City loaded a cannon with every St. Patrick's Day themed item they sold and shot it into the room. The decor was overwhelming but not tacky. Surprisingly, I liked it.

I leaned toward Liam, my curiosity overcoming my initial reluctance to show any interest in his life beyond tonight, and asked, "What's happening on Tuesday?"

Liam flashed me one of those stomach-twisting smiles and, though I refused to admit it, my knees might have wobbled a bit. "Ralph's kid has a hockey playoff."

"On a Tuesday?" I asked, lifting a brow. Curiosity was the feeling I needed to focus on, not the warmth and adoration that Liam would give up his Tuesday night to watch a friend's kid play hockey.

"Well, when you're six, the arena fits the games in wherever they can," he said with a chuckle, leading us toward the main bar across the room.

I wiggled through a maze of bodies, trying to keep up with Liam as he slipped effortlessly through the crowd. Rather than pushing through people for a spot at the front, Liam slipped behind the bar with practiced ease. He tapped the bartender on the shoulder. She jumped, almost dropping the drink she was mixing, and spun around.

"Liam!" she scolded, her voice carrying over the hum of the bar. She poured and garnished the drink, then handed it to the patrons who ordered. "You're not supposed to be here tonight."

"So I've been told, Amber," he replied, his expression boyish and unapologetic.

"It's your night off," Amber said, poking a finger at his chest. "You *promised* you wouldn't be here. What gives?"

Liam glanced at me briefly, the corner of his mouth twitching, before answering, "Needed a good drink. Figured this was the best place to get one."

Amber let out an exasperated groan and shook her head. "There are a million bars in this city, Liam."

"But none of them have you," he countered smoothly, his grin widening. "Now, if you won't make me something fabulous, I'll just have to do it myself."

Amber rolled her eyes, grabbed a glass from the cooler, and

placed it under the tap. "Your bar, your rules?" she muttered under her breath as she set to work on someone else's order.

"You're impossible," Liam teased, leaning casually against the counter. "What about you? Why are you here? I thought tonight was your night off."

"It was supposed to be," Amber admitted, looking slightly sheepish. "But Stephanie's birthday is coming up, and Chloe called out, and I figured I might as well cover the shift."

"Who's watching Stephanie?" Liam's voice softened, his teasing tone replaced with genuine concern.

"She's in the back," Amber said quickly, her words tumbling over each other. "I hope you don't mind. She's just sleeping, and she's not bothering anyone, and I check on her every thirty minutes. It's more than I would do if she were at home."

"Amber," Liam interrupted gently, holding up a hand. "Relax. You know Stephanie's always welcome here. She's the reason I remodeled the lounge next to my office. But you should've told me. I could've had someone watch her for you."

"I didn't want to bother you," she said, her shoulders easing slightly. "And she's fine. I set up a camera, so I can check on her if she moves. Besides, she was on her iPad until she fell asleep."

Liam's expression softened, and for a moment, I saw something unexpected: a side of him that wasn't just charm and wit. He genuinely cared about the people he worked with. I felt my lips lifting into a smile but quickly clenched my teeth to fight it. *Two hours.* I reminded myself. *In two hours Liam would forget I was ever a part of this night. I can't let myself get attached.*

"If you want to crash in the lounge after your shift, go for it," he said. "You're family."

Amber's shoulders eased as she gave him a grateful smile. "Thanks, boss. I better get back to work."

"Yeah, yeah," he said, waving her off before turning back to me.

"Boss?" I asked, folding my arms and arching a brow. There

was a playful edge to my voice, but my curiosity was genuine. "You own this place?"

He shrugged, downplaying the answer. "I might know a guy or two."

I narrowed my eyes, calling his bluff while trying to put the pieces together. And then it hit me. "Wait a minute. Your last name wouldn't happen to be *Smith*, would it?"

Liam's chuckle gave him away before he even nodded. "Guilty as charged."

"I think I know you," I said, the name finally matching up with the face. Excitement filled me with giddiness because I figured out who he was. "We had a class together in my first year of college. Right?"

"Western Civilization."

"I knew you looked familiar!" I declared triumphantly. Liam sat next to me every day until...

That excitement turned into lead as I remembered what happened between us. He found me on St. Patrick's Day and wished to go out with me. I rejected the wish because I actually liked the guy and couldn't stand the thought of him forgetting who I was.

He still ended up forgetting about me, only it was because he ignored me after that, not because my magic erased every conversation, text message, and coffee not-date. Life could be ironic. I tried so hard back then to keep those memories sacred, only for time to wipe them away.

"Hold on a second, doesn't your family own eight places around town? Why are you here with me instead of, oh, I don't know, finding a bride to save it all?"

Liam busied himself, grabbing a glass from the tray behind him and filling it with ice, his gaze deliberately avoiding mine. "Believe me, I don't want to lose Abbott's, but even if I do, I'd still be a partial owner, and depending on how much my brothers like me at the end of the day, I might even get to keep running it."

"Your brothers would let you stay?"

"Probably," he said, his grin turning crooked as he poured clear liquid into a mixing glass. "They'd be stupid not to run me into the ground as free labor. It's hard to say, but enough about me. Sweet or sultry?"

"Sweet," I answered automatically, watching as he expertly mixed a drink. "But this conversation isn't over."

"Good to know." Liam handed me the glass, his fingers brushing against mine for a brief moment that sent another flicker of heat through me. "Now," he said, leaning closer, "have you ever played Connect Four?"

I blinked. "What? Of course, I have. I was ten once."

"Perfect. There's a giant one out back," Liam said, his eyes sparkling with amusement and perhaps a little bit of challenge. "Care to play?"

"Wait," I asked, giving him a skeptical look. "This is your idea of fun?"

"This is my idea of breaking the ice," he said with a smirk. "Two hours, Holly. Don't judge me yet. I'm not the same man I was in college."

A smile tugged at the corners of my mouth despite myself. I liked the man I knew back then, and I had a feeling I'd like to know who he became if given the chance. It hurt to know that this was all we'd get, but I didn't have a choice. My magic had always been a double-edged sword. It gave me another chance with Liam just to rip that chance away.

I grabbed my drink and hopped off the stool. "Fine. Let's go."

Chapter 5

"Are you sure about this?" Liam asked, brow furrowing as he glanced at the Dance Dance Revolution screen. The arcade games were my favorite part of Abbott's. This was the only bar in town that offered something to do besides dance or drink, and since I rarely did either of those, I thoroughly enjoyed both times I came here. This game, in particular, was a favorite of mine.

"Positive," I said, tying my hair into a ponytail. "Why? Are you afraid of a little competition?"

"Afraid? No." Liam chuckled, stepping onto the platform. "Uncoordinated? Definitely."

The level started with an upbeat pop song I recognized from playing the game in the past but didn't actually know. After missing the first few steps and a split second of terror, I found my groove. My feet moved like they were on autopilot, hitting the arrows with precision and I was killing it. Liam, on the other hand, flailed like a fish out of water. For every five steps he took, he only managed to hit two.

I couldn't help but laugh, my breath hitching as I doubled over. Despite my amusement, I kept up every step. "Liam, you're *awful!*"

"No kidding," he replied, sweat forming on his brow as he stumbled again. "I think this machine's broken."

"Uh-huh," I teased. "Blame the machine."

By the time the song ended, I was breathless. My chest heaved as I stepped off the platform. Liam followed, panting ten times harder, like he'd just run a marathon. He bent over, hands on his hips, and just breathed for a solid ten seconds.

"Well, that was humbling," Liam said, standing upright. "I don't know how you made it look so easy."

"Growing up, Friday nights were spent at the mall, and let's just say I wasn't one of the popular kids in high school. My sister would be shopping or out on dates and I'd be in the arcade." I flashed him a grin that was one-third apologetic and two-thirds wicked. I had a feeling I would win the round, but I didn't think it would be by over ten thousand points. "Still, you weren't *half* bad."

"Liar," he shot back, a playful glint in his eyes. "But I'll take the compliment.."

We found an open table in the corner of the room, far enough from the dance machines to escape the noise but close enough to the bar that we weren't ignored. A server swung by to take our drink orders, and for the first time that evening, Liam looked completely at ease.

"You know," Liam said after a moment, swirling his drink, "tonight's the most fun I've had in ages."

I tilted my head, my curiosity piqued. "Really? You don't seem like someone who struggles to have fun."

"Let's just say life's been chaotic lately. The bet has been more taxing than I thought. Originally, it was all fun and games, but time is running out and..." he trailed off, a faint shadow passing over his features. But it disappeared as quickly as it came, replaced by his usual easygoing demeanor. "What now? We've got about an hour left."

I leaned back, considering. Liam was a great loser, but I didn't want to hurt his ego by wiping the floor with him again. I didn't trust myself to go somewhere more private with him, either. What to do... "What about Truth or Shot?"

Liam raised a brow. "Truth or Shot? I don't think I've played that since college."

"Same, but it's a classic. What do you think?"

"Alright." Liam stood up. "Wait here. I'll grab us something to drink."

I watched Liam swagger to the bar. Amber barely glanced at him but the other girls, the single ones looking for a fun time, barely took their eyes off him. He came back to me moments later with a bottle of tequila, two shot glasses, and a small plate of orange slices. I eyed the setup warily.

"Are you trying to get me drunk?" I asked, laughing nervously. I'd already had one drink tonight. Two would push me to tipsy, but shots would be a terrible idea. "I was thinking we could play with beer. Or at least something less potent than tequila."

"You're only at risk of drinking if you're terrible at answering questions," Liam teased, pouring the first shots. "Ladies first."

"Oh, how thoughtful," I said, picking up my glass with a mock sigh. "What do you want to know?."

Liam leaned back in his chair, a smirk playing on his lips. "What's the worst date you've ever been on?"

"Oh, you're going to *love* this," I began, dramatically emphasizing the word love. "So, I once matched with a guy on one of those dating apps. That was my first mistake—letting my sister sign me up. The second was agreeing to the date."

"So, why'd you go?"

I shrugged. "The guy was cute and I was in an epically long dry spell. At that point, I didn't care who the guy was or how we met. I just wanted a hook-up. Anyway, we had a normal dinner with way too many drinks and I didn't see the blazing red flags until it was too late. I let him take me back to his house, which turned out to be his parents' house."

"Oh, no."

"Just wait. It gets better. To which he decided to serenade me —and his parents—to the Youtube karaoke version of *I Wanna Fuck You* by Akon."

"No!" Liam shouts, practically dying with laughter. "Please tell me you're joking."

"Sadly, I'm not," I said, shaking my head. "Needless to say, I vowed never to go on one of those dating apps again, and I did not get laid. Your turn," I added, twisting my glass in my fingers. "What's one thing you've never told anyone?"

Liam hesitated, his easy demeanor faltering for a split second. "Sometimes I wish I wasn't tied to the family business. Don't get me wrong, I love our empire, but I wonder what life would be like if I wasn't constantly trying to live up to all the expectations. A part of me was grateful for the bet. My brothers have never taken me seriously, and really, I had nothing to lose. But then Abbott's deed was thrown into the pot, and well, you know the rest."

I studied him, amusement softening into something deeper. "I get that. There's an expectation my siblings and I will follow in our father's footsteps. He... uh... has a unique job and he's gone most of the year. Growing up, I thought I wanted to be like him. It was always the goal to get where he is, but I like my life. I don't know if I want that anymore," I confessed, surprising even myself.

Liam leaned back in his chair, thoughtfully tapping the rim of his shot glass. "Alright, Holly, my turn. What's the one thing you want you've never told anyone about?"

I paused, the question hanging between us like a dare. I rolled the shot glass between my fingers again, my gaze slipping to the table. "To be seen. Not as someone useful or convenient. Just... me," I said softly and then swallowed the tequila. It was strong but smooth. I let out a burning breath and met Liam's gaze. His brow furrowed slightly, but he didn't press the matter. Instead, he reached for the bottle and poured another round, keeping the mood light.

"Your turn," he said, gesturing for me to fire back.

I smirked, feeling a little lighter thanks to the liquor. "What's the most embarrassing thing that's ever happened to you?"

Liam groaned, shaking his head. "Why do I feel like I'm going to regret this?" He downed his shot and then sighed. "I needed that to tell this story. Let me set the scene. When I was sixteen, my brothers convinced me I was hilarious. So, for the high school talent show, I thought doing stand-up comedy would be a good idea. I figured it was no different than talking to our circle of friends, but when those spotlights hit me on the stage, I forgot all my jokes. In a moment of panic, I sang 'Twinkle Twinkle Little Star' instead."

I burst out laughing, nearly spilling my drink. "You did not!"

"Swear on my life," he said, holding up a hand. "And I was *terrible*. The crowd booed me offstage. My mom still brings it up every Thanksgiving."

My laughter eased into a warm smile, and Liam's gaze lingered on me a little longer than it should have. "Here's a potentially less traumatizing question," he said, his voice dropping just slightly, the playful edge giving way to something softer. "What's the first thing you noticed about me?"

My cheeks warmed, the tequila making me bold. I met his eyes, my voice steady despite the flutter in my chest. "Your smile. It's... disarming. It always has been."

Liam's lips twitched into that very smile, the one that seemed to light up the space between us. "Good to know."

The air between us shifted, heating and crackling the longer we stared at each other. I picked up the bottle of tequila and refilled his glass, breaking the tension with a quick, nervous laugh. "Alright, your turn. What's the dumbest thing you've ever done?"

Liam burst out laughing, the sound warm and unrestrained. "Oh, that's easy. When I was fourteen, I jumped off a dock trying to impress a girl. Totally forgot I didn't know how to swim. The lifeguard had to dive in and pull me out while everyone watched."

I laughed so hard that I nearly snorted. "No way. Did it work? Did you get the girl?"

"Not even close," he said, grinning. "She ended up dating some guy who knew how to paddleboard."

"My turn." Liam twisted the glass in his fingers. He seemed nervous, but he didn't look away. "Why'd you reject me all those years ago? I thought there was something between us."

There was. "Ouch. going deep with that one." I took my shot but didn't chase it with a slice of orange. I wanted the fire in my throat to burn away these feelings. Nervousness. Excitement. Nostalgia and... desire. "Don't take it personally. I haven't dated anyone since I was seventeen, at least not anyone I could see myself with for more than one night."

"So, you rejected me because you liked me?"

Yes. I filled my glass again and swallowed my shot as soon as I set the bottle down. "I believe it's my turn. Save that question for later."

For the next thirty minutes, we went back and forth, asking each other questions that spanned from simple things like how do you like your coffee all the way to embarrassing stories from our teenhood. The questions blurred and I began opting for shots over answers, letting the liquor speak when words wouldn't come. By the final round, I was laughing too hard to answer properly. My cheeks flushed from both the tequila and from how much I didn't want the night to end. I really, *really* liked spending time with Liam.

I pushed my glass away with a definitive shake of my head. "That's it. Game over," I declared, my voice a mix of amusement and resignation. "Any more and I'll be a disaster."

Liam raised his hands in surrender, his smile easy and warm. "Fair enough. You held your own longer than I expected."

"Damn right I did," I said, grinning, though my words slurred a little. I leaned back in my chair, the tequila's hazy heat spreading through me, and watched Liam pour himself one last shot. He downed it with a smoothness that suggested he wasn't nearly as affected as I was.

"Alright, champ," he said again, breaking the silence as he stepped closer. "What's next?"

I exhaled, the night air cooling my flushed cheeks. "It's almost midnight, which means your time is just about up and I should probably head home."

Liam nodded, his easygoing smile dimming only slightly. "Fair enough, but I'd never be able to live with myself if I put you in a car alone like this. Let me help you get home."

"I'll be fine."

"I insist. You're a great girl. I want to make sure nothing bad happens to you."

"All right," I said, trying to sound a little put-off and defeated when really I loved how considerate Liam was. I stood, wobbling a little, and he set his hand on my hip to steady me. I bit my lip and begged the swarm of butterflies tearing up my insides to settle. "Who am I to argue with a gentleman?"

As we stepped outside, the crisp air bit at my skin. It was refreshing but sobering. My mind raced with the realization that I was in my last moments with Liam. Soon, he'd forget who I was, and even though it was probably a bad idea, I wanted every minute I could get with him. Liam raised a hand to flag down a car, and within moments, we were tucked inside, the quiet hum of the engine filling the space between us.

The car ride was different from the bar's lively energy— quieter, charged with something unspoken. I stole a glance at Liam, who seemed content staring out the window, his profile outlined by the flickering lights passing by. He didn't press me for more conversation, and he didn't try to fill the silence, which was surprisingly relaxing.

I rested my head on his shoulder and tried to commit his scent to memory. I closed my eyes, and before I knew it, the car had stopped, and I was home. Liam paid the driver before I could protest and I murmured, "Thanks," while stepping onto the sidewalk.

He followed, standing close enough to feel his presence but not crowded, then asked, "Can I walk you up?"

I shook my head, a small smile tugging at my lips. "The rule still stands. I'm not sleeping with you."

"Even if you changed your mind, I wouldn't let you."

"Uh-huh. Sure." Though even as I mocked him, I could tell it was true. Sadly, it had crossed my mind to invite him inside, but things would get awkward if I rushed him into bed and he forgot who I was mid-stroke. I stuck my key in the lock and opened the door, the thought of us spending the night together a lingering battle I knew better than to let win.

"Scouts honor," he replied, holding up two fingers, his expression mockingly serious.

My laugh came easily, cutting through any awkwardness. The moment stretched as we stood there, his tall frame towering over mine, his hands tucked back into his jacket pockets as though he were restraining himself.

"Well, good night," I said, my hand resting on the doorknob, but just as I was about to step inside, something stopped me. I turned back, closed the space between us in a single breath, and kissed him.

It should have been soft, fleeting, and innocent, but instead, this kiss felt like its claws were sinking into my heart. My fingers brushed the curve of Liam's jaw, my lips pressing against his with a desperation I didn't mean to show, and he kissed me back just as ravenous. I wanted more than one night. I wanted to know what it would feel like to laugh with him again and to kiss him without the weight of magic pulling the strings.

But as I felt the threads of my spell unwinding, my heart sank. I knew this was all we would ever be. In less than a minute, Liam would forget me. The memory of the night would remain, but I would be erased from it like I'd never existed.

I pulled back and looked into his green eyes, committing every fleck of gold and every unspoken desire to memory. It was the last time I'd see him look at me like this.

"Thank you for tonight," I said softly, my voice trembling despite the small smile I forced to my lips. "I really enjoyed it."

"Me too," Liam replied, his brow furrowing slightly. "Can I see you again?"

I cupped his cheek, my thumb brushing against the faint stubble as tears stung my eyes. I couldn't answer him. Not truthfully.

"Goodbye, Liam," I whispered, letting the weight of the words settle between us before stepping inside and closing the door. I leaned against it, my chest heavy and my heart aching. My fingers trembled as I pulled my phone from my purse to look at the time. **12:02.**

The spell was done. My magic was gone for an entire year. I should have felt rejuvenated, like a flower finally kissed by the sun after too long in the shade.

But all I felt was regret.

The lingering ache refused to fade as I stared down at my phone. I scrolled to Dahlia's name, my lips pressing into a thin line. My sister had meddled tonight—she had to have. It was the only explanation as to why my chest felt tight and for why Liam's touch lingered like an ember refusing to die.

I hovered my thumb over the call button, hesitant to reach out this late. Whatever Dahlia had done to me, I wanted it undone. I needed this feeling gone before it consumed me.

Chapter 6

LIAM

I spent the next week trudging through work in a fog. Every time I tried to focus on my tasks, my mind drifted to Holly. My gaze would wander to the dancing game in the corner of the bar or to the rows of tequila bottles, and suddenly I'd be drowning in memories—her laughter, the way her lips brushed against mine and the electric spark that had followed. I wrestled with myself constantly, knowing exactly where she lived but unwilling to show up unannounced and risk coming across as a total creep.

At night, I stuck to my routine—throwing myself into every aspect of the bar, making the rounds with staff, and greeting regulars. But instead of scoping out potential candidates to fulfill the absurd bet my brothers had devised, I found myself scanning the crowd for brown hair and blue eyes. Each night I left without seeing her, the pit in my stomach grew heavier.

By the end of the week, Amber, the only person in the bar besides Ralph who had met Holly, had enough. "I'm tired of your moping."

"I'm not moping," I barely glanced up from the inventory sheet I'd been staring at for the past hour. I'd struggled and failed to track how many bottles we had on hand. Counting turned into thinking, which turned into remembering and every time I thought I'd dug myself out of the Holly rabbit hole I realized I'd fallen back in.

"Moping, sulking, drowning in sorrow—whatever you want to call it," Amber crossed her arms and leaned against the counter with a dramatic sigh. "You're basically a walking cliché of 'my heart was broken,' except your heart can't be broken because you just met the girl."

"I never said my heart was broken," I muttered, the words feeling heavy in my throat as I shifted uncomfortably in my seat. And I didn't just meet Holly. Fate threw my college crush back into my life at an impossible moment. But I didn't tell her that.

"Well, you're acting like it," Amber stepped forward and set a hand firmly on mine, forcing me to meet her piercing gaze. "You know where she lives. Either go find her or let whatever this is go. Those are your choices, Liam. But the clock is ticking. You're running out of time to win this bet—and let's be real, your brothers definitely haven't played fair."

I frowned, finally paying attention and looked up at her. "What do you mean?"

"Oh, please." Amber rolled her eyes, the exasperation in her tone impossible to miss. "The first week they sabotaged every girl you talked to by telling every single girl at the bar you had herpes. Don't even get me started on week two's rumors. They want you to fail, and I'm starting to think you do, too, because if you like Holly as much as you clearly do, you'd have made a move by now. Unless you want to give all this up."

"You know I don't want that." I dragged a hand through my hair and dropped onto a stool. "It's just...I don't know. I haven't felt this way about a girl in a long time. I can't get her off my mind."

"Then stop sitting here like an idiot and do something about it. She kissed you, right?"

"Well...yeah," I admitted, my ears heating at the memory.

"Then she's already opened the *we should be more than friends* door," Amber said with a knowing smile. She tilted her head as if the solution was painfully obvious and I was an idiot. "The least you can do is step inside and see what happens."

"You mean have it shut in my face," I muttered. I groaned and stared up at the ceiling when I finally looked at Amber again. She was staring at me. Waiting for me to man up. "I don't know anything about her except where she lives."

"Exactly! Holly let you take her home. It doesn't matter that you didn't get to go inside because girl code dictates that that's a neon flashing sign saying, 'Hey, I like you, but I don't wanna rush things.'"

"And the marriage clause of my bet would be rushing things."

"Tomato tomahto." Amber grinned, clearly pleased with herself. "Start small with flowers, or coffee, or maybe tequila. Whatever you think works. Worst-case scenario? She turns you away, and you'll finally stop pining. Best case scenario, she whisks you upstairs and you have mind numbing sex. Either way, you're in better shape than you are now."

Her words settled in my chest like a challenge, sparking a flicker of determination I hadn't felt in days. "You're right."

Amber blinked, her brows shooting up in surprise. Clearly, she hadn't expected me to actually take her advice. "Wait, you're really going to do it?"

"I'm gonna do it!" I said with a determined nod.

"Good." A slow, approving smile spread across her face. "Now get out of here and go get your girl."

I passed Holly's house three times before mustering up the courage to park the car. I stepped out with a bouquet of daisies in one hand, a bottle of tequila, and a bag of oranges in the other. I felt ridiculous—unsure whether this was the best or worst decision I'd ever made—but I was already here and Amber would roast my nuts if I chickened out.

With a deep breath, I knocked on the door. My heart thundered in my chest with each passing second. I questioned, for the hundredth time, if showing up was sweet or stalkerish. Part of me felt like if things had gone as well as I thought they did, Holly would have come back to the bar or at least given me her number. The other part of me hoped she was just busy or shy, or maybe just as nervous to see me as I was her.

The door eventually opened and Holly's blue eyes widened in surprise. "Liam? What are you doing here?"

I had a speech planned, one that made me sound suave yet sweet. But the moment I laid eyes on her I forgot everything. My speech. My name. What day of the week it was? My brain was an empty vortex, unable to form a single thought beyond, *damn she's gorgeous.*

After a painfully awkward minute, I remembered what words were. Although, what came out of my mouth was clunky, rushed and miles away from suave.

"These are for you," I said, holding out the daisies. My hand felt clammy, but I managed to hold the stems tight and not drop them at her feet.

Holly's lips parted slightly like she was shocked. She blinked, probably unsure what to make of me and the gesture. After another long moment, she reached out and took the flowers. "Thank you."

"I was hoping..." I began awkwardly, then cleared my throat and shifted my weight from one foot to the other. "I was hoping you'd want to get a drink. But if you don't want to go out, I, uh, brought tequila. No pressure, though. I just wanted to see you again."

Holly studied me, her gaze curious but guarded. "You did?"

"Yeah," I admitted, rubbing the back of my neck. This was going well... I think. Holly hadn't slammed the door in my face yet, so maybe Amber was right. Maybe there was hope for us and I spent the last week stressing over nothing. "I had a great time with you the other night, and I hope maybe you did too."

"You remember that night?"

"I wasn't that drunk," I said with a chuckle, trying to lighten the tension hanging in the air.

"Sorry, I just... I didn't think you'd remember me." Her words came out hesitant, as though she was afraid to hear my answer.

"Remember you? How could I forget you?"

Forgetting Holly was impossible. I'd tried, but she had a way of leaving a hole in your heart that no one but her could fill. Her rejection freshman year crushed me. I hoped tonight wouldn't be as painful.

Holly hesitated, her expression shifting between uncertainty and something else I couldn't quite place. Finally, she stepped back and opened the door wider. "Do you want to come in?"

"Yeah," I said, trying not to sound overly excited as I wiped my boots on the mat and stepped inside.

Her living room was cozy, with a cat tree in the corner and soft throws draped over the couch. Through the sliding door I saw a large hutch on the patio and two fuzzballs running around. I smiled at the sight, because what adult has guinea pigs? They live nearly as long as dogs. I assumed she got them as a child or maybe an early teen and has been caring for them ever since.

"I told you they'd miss me if you murdered me," she teased when she caught me looking at the cage.

"Good thing this isn't some intricate phase of my plan," I shot back with a grin.

To the right, in the kitchen, Holly set the tequila and oranges on the counter before rummaging through a cabinet for a vase. Her movements were quick, as though she was trying to distract herself. "Can I get you something to drink?"

I understood how she felt. I hadn't been this nervous to hang out with a girl since... well, I couldn't remember when. My stomach was so tumultuous, the idea of putting anything inside it was terrifying. The last thing I wanted was to throw up and ruin the small impression I might've made.

"So, how have you been?" Her gaze was fiercely focused on the bouquet. She cut the stem of each at an angle and carefully set each flower in the vase.

Confused. Lost in thoughts of her. Replaying college memories I'd forgotten. "Okay, I guess".

"Did you find a wife yet?" she asked, her tone light but her eyes cautious as they flicked up to meet mine.

I shook my head.

"That's a shame." The flowers were all set. The vase filled and on the counter. With nothing left to distract her, Holly had no choice but to pierce me with her pretty blues. "Just so you know, I'm not going to marry you."

"I wasn't going to ask," I said quickly, holding up my hands in mock surrender.

"Good." She laughed softly, the sound was enough to cut through the tension building between us, but her expression shifted. Her brows knitted together the same way they did when we studied together and she couldn't find an answer. "So why are you here, really? I mean, I'm happy to see you, but I'm confused."

"I wanted to ask you on a date," I said, my voice steady. "It doesn't have to be tonight. Whenever you're ready."

Holly bit her lip. "I don't know. You're trying to get married. Doesn't dating me seem a little pointless?"

"Not to me." Time with Holly had never and would never be pointless. My biggest regret is letting my bruised ego come between us. I spent the last six weeks of that Western Civilizations class staring at the back of her head because I was too much of a coward to talk to her. After that semester, we never had another class together. By the next semester, I'd gotten over my feelings, but not her. I wanted to apologize for being such a jerk and fix our friendship, but her number had changed and I never saw her again.

Holly sighed and folded her arms over her chest. "I don't think dating is a good idea, but we could be friends."

"I'll be whatever you let me be, Holly," I replied softly, the honesty in my voice surprising even me.

"Okay." Holly brushed her hands on her jeans and tilted her

head toward the living room, a small, tentative smile on her face. "Friends watch movies. Right?"

I grinned, even though the word *friends* stung more than I'd like to admit. I didn't want to be her friend. I wanted to tuck her hair behind her ears. I wanted to cup her cheek and taste her cherry-red lips. I wanted everything and anything she'd give me because she's all I've thought about since we found each other again. But I'd take what I could get. "Yeah, friends watch movies."

"Perfect. You pick something." She walked into the living room and grabbed the remote off the coffee table. She set it on the counter beside me, then walked around me to the kitchen again. She opened the pantry and said, "I'll make popcorn. Don't pick anything boring."

Because that's not a loaded task. Everything I like, she might hate. I scoured my memories, trying to find a clue that could help, but if she ever talked about movies or even a book that information was gone. I grabbed the remote and frowned at the TV. My thumb hovered over the buttons while the streaming app loaded.

I scrolled through the options, feeling the weight of every decision. If I picked a movie that was too romantic, would she think I was trying too hard? But if I picked an action movie, would she call me lame and predictable? I eventually landed on a rom-com about a guy and a girl who decide to be each other's dates for the holidays. I'd caught bits of it in the bar when Amber put it on during a slow afternoon, and the little I saw wasn't bad. *Safe enough, right?* I pressed play just as Holly returned with a bowl of freshly popped popcorn.

"Oh, I love this one," she said, her face lighting up with a genuine smile as she plopped onto the couch.

Her approval felt like a victory and I exhaled a small sigh of relief before sinking into the couch cushions. As the movie started, we both reached for the popcorn at the same time. Her fingers brushed mine, and the warmth of her touch sent a jolt straight up my arm.

Was that on purpose? No, probably just coincidence. But what if it wasn't? Should I scoot away and give her more space? Would staying put make things weird?

I stayed where I was, close enough to that our fingers bumped occasionally when we both reached for a handful. Sometimes, her arm would brush against mine and our shoulders would touch when she laughed. Each touch was like a spark, pulling my focus away from the screen no matter how hard I tried to focus on the movie.

Halfway into the movie, the leads were bickering, their chemistry undeniable, and I couldn't help but wonder if it was some kind of metaphor for us. Was this what we could be? Or was I just reading into things?

When the movie ended, Holly leaned forward to set the empty bowl on the coffee table. She turned to me, her voice soft but final. "Well, this was nice."

I hesitated, searching her face for any hint of what she might be feeling. There was nothing readable. I stared into her eyes, trying like crazy to decide what the next step should be. I didn't want to leave, but I refused to be a creep who overstayed his welcome and I doubted a night out was on the table. So, I had to accept that this was the end. "Can I see you again?"

"Liam..." Holly's easy smile faltered and her gaze dropped to her hands. "I don't know. I like you more than I should, but I can't get involved when you're supposed to be out there finding a wife. For the sake of Abbott's I hope you meet someone, but if things don't work out, you should come find me when the bet is done. Until then, I don't think it's a good idea for us to see each other."

My stomach dropped like a stone. I'd known this was coming. I had a feeling Holly wasn't the type to get tangled up in my mess, but hearing the rejection still hit like a punch to the gut.

"After the bet," I repeated, trying to keep the disappointment from creeping into my voice.

That would be three months from now. Could I really wait three months to see her again? Better yet, was I already considering throwing the bet just to see her again?

Holly nodded. "If this thing between us is real, Liam, I need it to be...clean. Not tied up in sibling chaos or a bet. You understand, right?"

"I understand." I stood and Holly walked me to the door. The distance growing between us felt heavier with each step. I paused at the threshold, my hand gripping the frame as I turned to look at her. "For what it's worth, I really like you, too."

Her lips curved into a bittersweet smile. "I figured, which is why we can't see each other. It's not fair to you. You need to save your bar, but I can't marry you. I'm sorry."

I nodded, stepping out into the cool night air. I couldn't shake the finality I felt in my chest. Even if I forfeited everything right now, I knew walking away would be the end of us and I wasn't ready to let go. "Before I go, can I get your number?"

Holly hesitated and gave me a worried look.

"You said we shouldn't see each other. That doesn't mean we can't talk every now and then. We're friends. Remember?" I was practically begging, she had to see it, but I didn't care. I let her slip through my fingers once and nearly lost her forever. This time, I was going to hold onto whatever tattered rope I could get.

"Sure." Holly held her hand out and I gave her my phone. She quickly typed in her contact information. When she handed it back, she whispered, "Bye, Liam," and let the door close, leaving me standing alone on her porch.

Chapter 7

LIAM

I laid in bed, staring at the ceiling fan, unable to sleep like I had every night since walking away from Holly last weekend. Images of her pretty face danced in my head, vivid and unrelenting—the way her laughter bubbled up during the movie, catching me off guard with its sweetness; the soft curve of her smile when our hands brushed in the popcorn bowl. The vulnerability in the eyes when she said she liked me.

She was a drug and I was thoroughly addicted. I thought texting would be enough of a fix and, for the first few days, it was but as the week dragged on I wanted more. I needed to hear her say something beyond the words that echoed in my mind. *"Come find me when the bet is done."*

I groaned, rolled onto my side, and yanked the pillow over my head. Come find her. That single sentence haunted me.

What did she mean by that?

The more I thought about it, the more I realized that it wasn't a rejection—not outright. But it wasn't an invitation either. It was... conditional. A *maybe*, dangling between us like a loose thread I didn't know how to tie.

I squeezed my eyes shut and sighed. It wasn't fair—this ache, this pull to be near her. I flopped onto my back again and hugged the pillow with both hands. My heart thudded unevenly as my thoughts spiraled. This stupid, fucking bet was ruining my life.

What should have been a chance to prove that I was more than the idiot little brother who was only useful behind the bar, had turned into something so much bigger. Something I hadn't planned for.

The rules had been simple: charm a pretty girl into marrying me and they'd each hand over ten percent of their shares. I'd have the most swing when it came to the family business. My brothers would have no choice but to listen and respect my opinions and I'd finally be more than just the baby brother bartender.

The family fuck up.

At the time, the stakes felt so trivial. I literally had nothing to lose. Monetarily, ten percent was a drop in a hat. I was in this for the respect, not the money, but then things got heated and I threw the deed to Abbott's into the pot to prove I was taking the opportunity seriously.

And I was...

Until Holly walked back into my life.

I groaned again, realizing but not wanting to admit I would risk everything that I was fighting for for her. Was that crazy? We barely knew each other.

A moment from the first night we met flashed through my mind and all I could see was her. Her smile. The way she tilted her head when she was trying to hide her curiosity. The guarded look in her eyes that told me she felt just as much as I did, but was scared of getting hurt.

I wouldn't hurt her. In fact, I had this strange urge to protect her. I wanted her to curl up beside me so I could hold her and tell her I'd never let anyone hurt her again. I wanted to be her rock, the anchor to the lifeboat she hadn't stepped into yet. And that was my problem.

I was gone for a girl who wasn't even sure if she wanted me in her life.

I jolted up, the tension that had kept me rooted in bed gone, replaced with a nervous energy that demanded action. Sleep was pointless. I knew what I needed to do, and lying here wasn't going to make it happen.

Early morning air carried the faint scent of dew and the promise of hope. In a few hours the sun would burn off the last tendrils of winter, but for the next hour or two the outside world was cool, calm, and collected.

The complete opposite of how I felt.

I glanced down at the tissue wrapped bouquet I picked from the flower cart on the corner of eighth and first street. My confidence wavered as I questioned, again, whether showing up with them was a good idea or not. I'd given Holly flowers the last time we were together. Were two bouquets too much? Did they show that I cared, or did they scream desperation?

Last night, while I was planning this, they felt like a nice gesture. Now, I wasn't sure, but I was committed. With a deep breath, I forced myself not to throw them into the bushes and knocked on her door. My heart thudded in the pause that followed.

The door eventually creaked open and Holly appeared, blinking at me in surprise. She wore a loose sweatshirt and leggings, her hair piled into a messy bun that somehow made her look even more beautiful in her natural, unpolished way.

"Liam?" she asked, her voice still thick with sleep.

"Good morning." I lifted the bouquet slightly, a sheepish smile tugging at my lips. The flowers were lame. I should have brought donuts. Everyone loves donuts! But if I had brought donuts, it would have ruined my plan... My thoughts spun in circles, so before I could stray from what I'd devised and make any more of a fool of myself than I already had, I said, "These are for you. I thought they might brighten your day."

Holly's eyebrows arched as her gaze dropped to the flowers. For a moment, she just stared at me, as if she were trying to figure out why I was on her porch so early on a Sunday morning. It really was early, barely eight AM and I could tell I'd woken her.

Just as I was about to apologize for showing up unannounced, a slow, soft smile spread across her face. She reached for the bouquet, her fingers brushing mine. "Daisies and lavender. These are my favorites."

"Lucky guess," I said, though, in truth, I'd spent nearly fifteen agonizing minutes at the flower cart, overthinking every option until I finally committed. Holly's bathroom had a lingering aroma of lavender, so I thought there was a good chance she'd like the stems. As for the daisies, those were my mother's favorite. I figured she wouldn't steer me wrong and so I paired the two together. Plus, I liked the way the purple and white looked together.

"Do you want to come inside? I just made a fresh pot of coffee."

"I'd love to." I slid my shoes off near the door and followed the familiar path to the kitchen. It felt like deja vu. I was following in last week's footsteps, only today I was going to take that needle pointing at *friends* and push it one tick closer to *more*.

Holly set the flowers on the kitchen counter then rummaged through a drawer for another vase. Last week's stems were still alive, a little wilty, but she hadn't tossed them yet. "So, what brings you by so early? Shouldn't you be sleeping after working last night?"

"I'm a morning person," I said casually, leaning against the counter. To some degree I was, even after late nights, but I usually wasn't up *this* early. "And I thought maybe we could grab some breakfast from KeKe's in town. Unless you're busy?"

Holly's hands paused at the faucet, just before filling the lemonade pitcher she grabbed in place of a vase. Her blue eyes darted up and she looked at me as if she were trying to peer into my soul. "Breakfast, huh?"

"Yeah," I said, my tone deliberately light. "Nothing fancy. Just two friends satisfying the completely normal urge to eat."

She filled the pitcher with water and opened the little packet of powder marked flower food. I waited patiently as she created the mixture and then watched her add the stems. She clipped and set each one with precision. Those piercing eyes flicked to me every few minutes, curious if I was still watching. I was and I wasn't ashamed that I liked what I saw.

Five minutes that seemed to stretch a lifetime while simultaneously flying by passed before she said, "Okay. Let me just run upstairs and get dressed."

"Take your time." I shoved my hands in my pockets to keep from reaching out to her. I wanted to grab her by the wrist as she passed and pull her close. I wanted to taste those lips again and feel her warmth against my chest.

And I would, but not today.

I walked around the bottom floor of her duplex while I waited. Pictures of Holly and friends, perhaps even family, hung on the wall. I recognized Dahlia in one and wondered if the two other women in the photo were her sisters, too. They looked nothing alike, then again I never would have guessed Dahlia and Holly to be related had she not told me otherwise.

A few minutes later, Holly came down the steps in a pair of dark jeans and wrapped in a cozy sweatshirt. Her messy bun was still intact and somehow she looked effortlessly put together, like she hadn't tried at all, yet she still managed to make my pulse quicken.

"Ready?" I asked and she nodded.

Outside, I opened the door for Holly and waited as she stepped into my Honda Civic. I'd had the car since college and had never been self-conscious about it. It was paid off, something my brothers couldn't say about their high-end vehicles, which usually made me proud. But for the first time, I wondered if the older car made me look... I didn't know... less than.

The thought didn't linger long because as soon as I sat beside

Holly her sweet scent filled the space around us and I was officially high on a perfume buzz. I pulled out of the driveway, letting the radio play in the background for a few minutes. The silence between us wasn't awkward but it felt loaded, like she was waiting for me to say something first.

"So," I began, glancing at her from the corner of my eye. "What do you do these days? I'm ashamed to say I don't remember what your major was."

"I'm a marketing manager," Holly said, folding her hands in her lap. "I work from home most days, but I visit my clients in person once or twice a month. Emails and Zoom meetings are convenient, but it helps to actually see people face to face and get a feel for how things are going."

"That's cool," I said, genuinely impressed. "Do I know any of the companies you work for?"

"Probably," she replied with a hint of pride. "I've got accounts with Paws Groom and Board, Tony's Pizza, and Sarah's Sweet Treats."

"Sarah's?" I grinned. "I love that place. Their cinnamon rolls are legendary."

"Right?" Her eyes lit up and she relaxed a little. "It's dangerous having their menu samples lying around during brainstorming meetings. Last time, they brought out a whole pecan pie, and I single-handedly ate half of it before the end of the day."

I laughed, the mental image of Holly sneakily devouring pie far too endearing. "I bet Sailor would bring you on if she knew what you do."

"Who's Sailor?"

"She owns Keke's," I explained, turning onto the main road toward the café.

Holly's eyebrows rose in surprise. "Really? I would've thought Keke owned it."

"Nope," I said, shaking my head. "Keke's her daughter. Sailor opened the diner when Keke was eight so she'd have a legacy to pass down. Now Keke's the head waitress and will be assistant manager once she graduates high school."

Holly tilted her head, intrigued. "That's actually really sweet. You know a lot about them."

"I grew up with Sailor. There was a running bet for years which Smith son she'd end up with," I said with a shrug. "The answer, if you're curious, was none of us. I was two years too young and my brothers lost interest once she got knocked up."

Holly pulled out her phone, a glimmer of admiration in her eyes. "Her website has good traction, but it could be better. You think she'd be interested in working with a marketing manager?"

"Maybe. I can introduce you next week if you want," I offered casually, though I felt a surge of excitement at the idea of helping her land another client. Sailor was off today. She and Keke kept Sunday as a family day, but I now had reason for Holly to want to see me again.

Holly's hand slipped across the console, her fingers brushing mine before giving a gentle squeeze. "That would be great. Thanks, Liam."

She left them there, intertwined with mine the whole car ride. It wasn't until I parked and was forced to let her go did we separate. "Fair warning," I said as I opened the car door. "I've known Sailor's mom, Alice, since I was a kid."

Holly raised an eyebrow, her tone cautious. "Okay?"

I could tell she didn't quite understand, but as soon as we stepped inside the diner, her confusion began to clear. The moment Alice spotted me her face lit up as bright as the diner's neon sign. She tucked her notepad into her apron and hurried over, shooing away the hostess when she tried to greet us.

"Liam!" Alice pulled me into a tight hug that smelled faintly of flour and vanilla. "I swear, you get more handsome every time I see you."

I loved Alice. She was warm, and kind, and never made me feel like I was a burden. She took me under her wing after my mom died and offered me more guidance than my dad or our nannies ever offered. She was family. "Good to see you, too. How've you been?"

"Oh, you know. Just living my best life." Alice's sharp eyes darted to Holly. Unlike my brothers, I never brought girls to the diner. This place was sacred. It was natural for her to be curious, but also nerve-racking. Her big browns rolled over Holly with a mixture of hesitation and wonder. "And who's this pretty creature?"

Holly extended a hand, her smile widening. "I'm Holly. Nice to meet you."

Alice glanced at Holly's outstretched hand and waved it away, then pulled her into a quick but firm hug. "Honey, if you're here with this one, we hug, not shake." She patted Holly's back before stepping back, beaming at us both. "I bet you're hungry. Let me sit you at the best booth we've got. Follow me."

Alice guided us to a cozy corner booth meant for six, complete with vinyl seats that creaked as we slid in. The dinner had always been warm and cozy, but it felt even more special today. "Now, y'all look over the menu, and I'll be back in a jiffy with two glasses of water."

As she walked away, Holly turned to me, bright-eyed. "She's delightful."

"I tried to warn you," I said, shrugging as I leaned back in the booth.

Holly shook her head, laughing softly. "Your warning did *not* count as a warning. It was like a bike bell when a train horn was needed." She grinned, picking up the laminated menu. "But I like Alice. She's sweet."

After giving us a few minutes to read over the menu, Alice returned with water and a notepad in hand. Holly ordered eggs Benedict, while I went with my usual French toast casserole. Once she left, Holly leaned her elbows on the table, her gaze steadily on me.

"So, what are you going to do about that bet?"

"At this rate?" I expected a sting in my chest at the realization that it was over, but something in me changed last night. I was at peace with letting Abbott's go. My brothers will expect me to keep running it—and I will... until I can open Abbott's 2.0 somewhere else. My staff are loyal to me, not the family brand, so the ones that matter will move with me. It'll take some time, but everything will be alright. "Lose. But I've come to terms with it."

Her expression faltered, a small frown tugging at the corners of her lips. "You can't! There has to be something you can do. A loophole. Maybe?"

I shook my head. "No loopholes. The chances of meeting a girl and having her fall head over heels in love in a little over two months is slim. I'd be better off switching my focus to what's next. Abbott's isn't successful because of the games, it's the people. My team will move with me. I just have to figure out where I'm going."

"I could help with the marketing. I feel bad because there's something between us but marriage is... it's just...." Her words trailed off and she reached out and touched my arm, giving it a sympathetic squeeze. "I'm sorry, Liam."

I covered her hand with mine and gave her a small, reassuring smile. "It's okay. Honest. Besides, I didn't bring you here to talk about my problems."

Her head tilted slightly and she leaned back, pulling away the warmth of her touch. "So, why *did* you bring me here?"

I met her gaze, the corner of my mouth lifting into a half-smile. "Because we're friends." I emphasized that last word, making it known that we may be friends but hopefully not for long. Not if I could help it. "And I was hungry. I figured you might be, too."

Holly's cheeks turned the coziest shade of pink. She shifted on the cushion and scooted closer to me. There was so much I wanted to say, but I was walking a careful line. Our friendship was in a delicate state. One push too hard and I could lose everything.

"I'm curious..." Holly said to herself, pulling out her phone.

She scrolled until our breakfast came, muttering little *oh*s and *hmm*s, but I didn't mind. It took the pressure of trying to figure out what to say away. I'd planned everything down to a tee, except this part. I grilled her about her job already. I didn't want breakfast to teeter into awkwardness. Besides, long-term couples don't talk every minute they're together. They have to learn how to coexist in the quiet spaces. I liked to think this was the first of many moments like this and that we were rocking it.

When the food arrived, Holly's eggs Benedict looked picture-perfect, while my French toast casserole was every bit as indulgent as I remembered. We both dove in hungrily devouring each bite.

"This is *amazing*," Holly said between mouthfuls, her eyes lighting up as she savored her meal.

"Alice knows what she's doing," I said, spearing a piece of my casserole with my fork.

That was all the conversation we had. Holly was too busy savoring every bite and I enjoyed watching her. By the time we left, the sun was high in the sky, casting a golden glow over the street. It was nearly mid-morning and if I was honest, I was starting to feel the wear of not sleeping last night.

The drive back to Holly's house was quieter than the ride over, but it wasn't uncomfortable, Just peaceful. When we pulled into her driveway, Holly lingered on the porch after I walked her to the door. I could tell she wanted more, just like I did last time I was here, but I was teetering on exhausted. If I were to sit on her couch for too long I'd probably fall asleep.

"Thanks for today," Holly said, her voice soft. "Do you want to come in?"

I hesitated, the invitation tempting, but I shook my head. "I'd love to, but I should probably get going."

"Oh." There was a flicker of disappointment on her face that gutted me. I almost said *fuck it,* but then she quickly added. "I enjoyed this. Maybe we could hang out again sometime?"

"Absolutely," I said, grinning. "I'll text you later."

"Okay." Her smile turned playful, almost hopeful and I couldn't help the rush of excitement I felt.

I started to back away and believe me it was the last thing I wanted to do. Top of the list of what I wanted was to kiss her goodbye, middle of it was take a nap, then go to Abbott's and finish that inventory list I was supposed to have finished two weeks ago. Of the three, I was committing to the latter. I needed to stay busy. As far as my brothers were concerned, everything would carry on as expected.

Until I was ready for them to know otherwise.

Chapter 8

HOLLY

> Liam: What do you call a fish wearing a bowtie?

> Me: I'm sorry, what?

> Liam: What do you call a fish wearing a bowtie?

> Me: Oh, gosh. This is one of your jokes. Isn't it?

I stared at my phone, smiling. Two minutes. Liam had been gone for less than two minutes, and he was already texting me. I liked it more than I probably should. Letting myself like Liam was dangerous.

> Liam: Humor me,

> Me: Alright. What?

> Liam: Sofishticated.

The joke was so stupid, but I laughed, the sound surprising me. It bubbled out of me in a way I couldn't control, warm and genuine. I pressed my phone to my chest, letting the moment linger. It was a silly, ridiculous joke, but it was so him. Thoughtful, sweet, always trying to make me smile. Just like I remembered.

I closed my eyes and savored the weightless, giddy feeling that came over me whenever Liam texted.

Out of all my sisters, I liked to think I was the practical one. River's mood changed with the wind. Autumn wanted to fix the world. And Dahlia was... well, Dahlia; always inserting herself into people's lives without warning.

Whereas I was the glue of the family, the level-headed one when chaos came out to play. With my magic accessible only one day of the year, I lived a mostly normal life—unlike my siblings—and often had to do damage control when their mischief didn't go as planned. Then, when mom died, I stepped into the "watchful eye" roll and made sure life kept going. River stayed in school, though it took a lot of convincing. Dahlia kept her job in finance despite wanting to drop everything to start a dating app. And Autumn... well, the goal had and probably would always be to keep her out of jail. That girl had a wild streak that got her in trouble more days than not.

The point was that I was one hundred percent *not* the type to lose myself to a boy after one *maybe* date. That was Dahlia's m-o. And yet here I was, my back pressed against the cold door, my stomach alive with butterflies, my heart racing like I'd just run a marathon and my cat... well Daisy had every right to be side eyeing me.

"Don't look at me like that."

Her head tilted a fraction of an inch and she let out a single *meow* in response.

I know. I agree.

Liam was going to be trouble. He was handsome, kind, and determined. From what I could tell, he checked all of my could-we-be-a-match boxes. He was the kind of guy I would want if I were looking for a relationship, not a hookup.

I chewed on my thumbnail, my lips lifting slightly, until I remembered everything that was on the line for Liam. I sighed and pushed off the door. He might be the one for me, but I wasn't the right girl for him. I couldn't be. My magic would make me flirt with people every year to earn their secrets and that's not something you do when you're in a relationship, let alone married.

Nope. Until I found my soulmate and gave my gift up, I was forced to be single.

I bent down to pet Daisy as I ambled to my room, but she ran away and hid behind the sofa. Typical cat. Judge me but don't have the gaul to face the consequences.

Around lunchtime, my phone dinged and I was painfully surprised at how disappointed I felt when I realized it was just Dahlia lighting up the family group text and not Liam.

Dahlia: Alright bitches you know what day it is. Who's bringing what tonight?

Autumn: I've got dessert: strawberry cheesecake, cupcakes, and the lemon macaroons.

River: That's a random assortment. What's wrong?

Autumn: Nothing, I just felt like baking.

River: The only time you bake that much is when something is wrong.

Dahlia: She's right. Everything OK with you and Max?

River: We're fine. I just felt like trying out some new recipes.

Dahlia: Uh-huh, sure. Holly, you're awfully quiet. Are we still getting together at your house tonight?

Me: Yeah. Sorry. Just a little distracted. Tonight is great. How does pizza sound?

Autumn: We had pizza last time. How do you guys feel about lasagna? I can stop at Gio's and pick one up.

Me: It doesn't matter to me. I was just going for easy.

River: I like lasagna.

Dahlia: Cool, see you guys tonight, then. I love you bitches!

The rest of the day dragged. I vacuumed, mopped, and did the load of laundry that was sitting in my hamper. I scrubbed my bathrooms, cleaned the litter box, and by the time I looked at the clock, only two hours had passed. I groaned and fell onto my bed, then stared up at the ceiling.

Liam had invaded my thoughts so many times over the last two weeks, but after seeing him today it was becoming increasingly hard not to think about him and the singular dimple that came out of hiding when he smiled.

It was crazy how much I liked him. I knew he was a problem I needed to get rid of, but I'd never felt this way for someone before. Not even with Joe, the guy I lost my virginity to, and I would have sworn on the Bible that I loved him with all my heart. Or at least as much as a seventeen-year-old heart can love before you break up, go to college, and then find out he was cheating on you your whole relationship.

Joe was a jerk, but Liam is a sweetheart. If he was anything like the man I knew in college there was zero chance of Liam doing me dirty like that. I chewed on my lip, still trying to make heads and tails of this thing with him...me...us.

Dahlia already said she didn't meddle the night we met. She swore it, but I know her. Sometimes, if she gets even the tiniest inkling of a tingle, she'll give people who don't need a push a sprinkle of magic.

Half the time, though, Dahlia's inklings were *very* wrong. Like the time, we saw this couple, or at least these people she thought should have been a couple, at the mall. In her defense, they kept laughing and looking at each other with bedroom eyes. They had an essence where you could tell there was something between them but life was holding them back.

After fifteen minutes of stalking, she decided to give them a little magical push. The boy leaned over and kissed the girl. For one beautiful heartbeat, it seemed like everything was going to go smoothly, but then the girl slapped him across his face, and their mother turned to the corner and freaked the F out.

Turned out they were step-siblings. He might have had a massive crush on his sister, but from what we saw, the family did not approve. Which led me back to my dilemma. This crazy, mind-spinning, stomach turning, heart racing anxiety was what I imagined a love spell felt like.

And there was only one gentry in the tri-county area with the gift of love.

I grabbed my phone off the bedside table and called my sister. I needed to hear Dahlia say she didn't mess with my life. I needed to look her in the eyes and have her tell me what I felt was real. And this wasn't a conversation I wanted to have in front of my sisters.

The phone rang and rang, but she didn't answer. I sat up, chewing on my thumbnail, and then called her again. She still didn't answer. It was Sunday. I knew she wasn't working, so what the hell was she doing? Why wasn't she picking up?

About a minute later, my phone vibrated and Dahlia's face popped up on my screen. I swiped my thumb to answer the call, but now I was too fired up to sit still. My hands shook with anxious energy and there was a heaviness in my chest that only eased when I stood up.

"Are you dying?" Dalia asked, irritation dripping off her

words. She was in a grocery store with rows of cereal boxes behind her, which explained why she didn't answer.

Dahlia hated talking on the phone in public. She always said her conversations were personal, and even though bystanders could only hear one side—her side—she didn't like all the nosey Nellies in town.

"Are you sure you didn't meddle?" I asked, pacing my bedroom. The floor creaked under my bare feet, a sound that usually comforted me but now only added to my restlessness.

"Holly," Dahlia said with a sigh, but I could hear the amusement in her voice.

My life was funny. Great. Next time she had a crisis, you could bet your ass I was going to use this same light-hearted *life isn't this serious* tone.

"For the last time, no. Your love life is your business. I wouldn't interfere even if I wanted to—which I don't, by the way."

"Then how do you explain this?" I pressed, waving my hand to the empty air as though she could see the crazy, ooey-gooey feelings practically smothering me. "He remembered me, Dahlia. Even after midnight when I was supposed to be a hole in his mind. He remembered. That's not normal."

"Maybe this guy is your soulmate," she replied, her tone light but laced with something deeper. Her words hit me like a thunderclap, and I froze mid-step. My heart stuttered, then picked up in an uneven rhythm when she added, "Ever think of that? Maybe that's why he remembered you."

"My soulmate?" I repeated, my voice barely above a whisper.

"Why not?" Dahlia asked. "It makes sense. You're borderline obsessed. If you're calling me this much it's because you're thinking about him and that scares you. No one has ever scared you, Holly. Only one person could ever scare you."

I didn't respond right away. The idea settled over me like a heavy blanket, both comforting and suffocating. I didn't think my soulmate was real. I knew about the loophole, but I thought it was just one of those gentry tricks our kinfolk like to play. Lure innocent souls with a promise of release when really there was no chance in hell of getting out of whatever they agreed to.

My sisters and I agreed to nothing. We were born with our blessings that are also our curse.

But Liam remembered me. More so, he seemed to really want me.

To like me.

"Or," Dahlia added, her teasing tone returning, "he's just a really good guy who happens to remember pretty girls. Either way, you should enjoy yourself." She looked past me to someone in the store then said, "We can talk more at dinner, but I gotta go. Love you." And then she hung up.

I stuffed my phone into my back pocket and headed downstairs into the kitchen. My mind churned with possibilities as I rummaged through the fridge for something to eat for lunch. Enjoy myself? Did she even hear herself? I was not the kind of person who just threw caution to the wind. I planned. I evaluated. I kept things under control.

And yet, my heart raced just thinking about Liam—his dimpled smile, the warmth in his eyes, the way he'd looked at me like I was the only person in the world. It was too much. Too fast. Too... *perfect*.

"Damn it, Dahlia," I muttered, pulling out a bottle of water and slamming the fridge shut.

My sister's words replayed in my head. *Your soulmate.* The very idea sent my mind spinning. Was that what this was? Could it be? But how? Why now? And why him? My heart felt like it was racing to outrun my thoughts, a flurry of questions with no answers.

I pressed my palms flat against the cool countertop, taking deep breaths to steady myself. "This is insane," I whispered to no one but Daisy, who sat perched on the back of the couch, watching me with her usual feline judgment.

Her wide green eyes seemed to say, *Finally catching up to your feelings, huh?*

"Nope." I straightened, shaking my head like I could physically dislodge the thoughts threatening to overtake me. "Not tonight. I can't do this tonight."

I needed to focus on the here and now—like the fact that my sisters would be here in just a few hours, expecting pizza or lasagna and a spotless house. They didn't need to see me unraveling over a guy I barely knew, no matter how perfect his smile was.

Chapter 9

HOLLY

The lasagna was gone—every cheesy, saucy bite devoured amidst our tipsy laughter and the occasional outrageous shout over a *Cards Against Humanity* card. The growing lineup of empty wine bottles on the counter felt like a monument to our excellent choices, and the lingering scent of garlic bread was a warm reminder of the perfect dinner we destroyed.

River leaned back in her chair, a rosy flush tinting her cheeks, and threw down a card with a triumphant smirk. "This one is gold. Prepare to lose."

Dahlia read the card out loud, "*A middle-aged man on roller skates.*"

It shouldn't have been funny because it didn't even match the prompt, but the wine had worked its magic. I laughed so hard my stomach hurt, all while tossing down my own nonsensical response: *Grandma's last surprise party.*

"Okay, that's disturbing," River said, holding up her hands in mock surrender, her laughs coming through like breathy cackles. "You win. My bladder can't handle all this laughing anymore." She set her cards on the coffee table and hurried to the bathroom, still laughing as she shut the door.

"Wimp!" Autumn shouted, then turned to me with a grin. "Well, since that game is over. What should we do now?"

"Please don't tell me the night is over!" River shouted

through the bathroom door. She whipped it open, still zipping her jeans, and added, "We haven't had this much fun in ages."

I dropped my head back against the couch cushions and closed my eyes. The world moved around me, swaying from side to side, but I felt good. River was right; this was one of the best girls' nights we'd had in months. We skipped February's get-together. Dahlia's magic buzzed through her like an earthquake all month. She wouldn't have been able to relax even if she wanted to and January was rough because it was the anniversary of Mom's passing. Before that, there were the holidays, which carried their own kind of chaos. So, our last real girls' night was back in October.

I also wasn't ready to call it a night yet, but a small part of me wanted to be elsewhere. It was hard to focus on my sisters when I kept thinking about Liam. He was working again and I was itching to see him. Ideally, without my sisters, but outside of Dahlia, they'd be none the wiser if we ventured to a bar or two and happened to see Liam while we were out. "Do you want to go out for a drink?"

The room went dead silent, save for the soft clink of a wine glass being set down. A flush of panic raced through me. Maybe this was a bad idea. Maybe I should have faked a migraine and pretended to go to bed, then snuck out to see Liam. Oh, my god. What am I? Twelve? I wouldn't be sneaking out. This was my house. I owned it and lived by myself. I was a grown woman. I could do whatever or whoever I wanted, whenever I wanted!

I took a breath and forced a smile. Everything was fine. I was fine. This was just the alcohol panicking.

River gasped, clutching her chest like she was auditioning for a soap opera. "Who are you, and what have you done with my sister?"

Autumn squinted at me like she wasn't sure she'd heard me right. "You? Go out? Like, leave the house?"

Heat crept up my neck as my thoughts spiraled down a new, terrifying path. What if they hated Liam? Or worse...what if they liked him? Like really liked him! Would I have to explain who he was, or better yet, who he could be? Would I have to fight my sisters off and claim him as mine? Dahlia wouldn't be a problem; she could read a room, but Autumn was worse than a rabbit. She hooked up with more men in a month than I did my whole college career, and I practically lived on Tinder. River would back down as soon as she realized there was a competition. And I...

I was doing it again.

I grabbed a throw pillow and hugged it to my chest. My skin hummed with anxious energy ready to fight my sisters over a guy they didn't know existed. Something was seriously wrong with me. "It's just been a while since we've gone to a bar together. I think it could be fun."

Dahlia arched a brow, suspicion dancing in her eyes. "Fun? Who even are you?" She paused for a beat, the pieces probably clicking in place, then added, "Where?"

I hesitated, suddenly very aware of how much they were all staring at me. "I was thinking..." Ok. Here I go. I just needed to play the suggestion cool and sound aloof. I could do that. I was a strong, independent woman with some very cool, very rare lineage.

I had this in the bag.

"Abbott's." My voice betrayed me. It squeaked and then went all breathy, which was one hundred percent *not* aloof. I quickly added, "Unless there's somewhere else you'd rather go," and hoped I sounded less desperate.

River let out an audible gasp, louder and even more dramatic than before. "Abbott's? The bar with the hot bartenders and overpriced cocktails? Yes. Yes. Yes!"

Autumn leaned forward, her expression skeptical but amused. "If we weren't sitting in your house right now, I'd assume you'd been abducted and replaced by someone who actually knows what the word 'fun' means."

If she had been anyone but my sister, I might have been

offended, but Autumn was right. Fun was usually far from the top three words in my vocabulary. Work, family, and reading generally had the award-winning spots.

I stood, grabbing my purse and hoping that my newfound confidence—*or insanity*—would make up for my racing heart. "So, are we going or not?"

Dahlia shot me a look. She knew why I wanted to go to Abbott's and who I wanted to see. I could tell she knew. The question was, was she going to say anything? "Oh, we're going. There's no way I'm missing this."

* * *

The line outside Abbott's stretched around the block and around the corner. It was still early in the night, barely ten, but laughter and music spilled into the warm night air. I wrapped my arms around myself, despite it being in the mid-seventies, and tried to fight off a chill and my nerves.

What was I even doing here? I didn't do this. Unless it was St. Patrick's Day, I didn't go out to bars, and I damn sure didn't chase guys. If Autumn or River were to find out what I was actually doing at a place like this, I'd blame the alcohol. Its liquid courage nudged me to stalk a handsome man. Yup. That's what I'd say. I'd tell them my fuzzy thoughts followed a blurry path forged by an invisible string tied to the man who just happened to own Abbott's.

Dahlia would argue that this pull to be near Liam was more than a drunken desire, but I'm not ready to entertain that notion. Not yet. Not until I know more about him.

"Are you sure about this?" River asked, giving me a sideways look as we waited in line. "I don't think I've seen you willingly leave the house in the past eight years."

I rolled my eyes, but her comment hit closer to home than I wanted to admit. I didn't leave my house very often because I was comfortable there. I'd accepted what my magic meant for my life and made peace with it years ago. Plus, there was always someone willing to hook up on some app or another if I got lonely, which wasn't often.

"I'm sure," I said, but the longer we waited, the more my buzz faded. My confidence teetered into nervousness and I was starting to regret coming out. But we were here. There was no turning back. "Let's just get inside before I change my mind."

Thirty minutes later, we reached the front of the line. By this point, I was so nervous I was nauseous. I stood wedged between Dahlia and Autumn, who were in a lively conversation about her newest vibrator and how Autumn *had to get one.* We were at the front for less than a minute before the bouncer said, "Holly?"

I looked up, vaguely recognized him. "Uh, yeah?"

"I thought that was you. It's me... Ralph." The man touched his chest and beamed down at me. I remembered him now.

"How'd the game go last week?" I asked, and Ralph's face lit up. I'm sure he didn't expect me to remember the cryptic conversation with Liam, or to dig deeper into what they were talking about, but how could I not? It still makes me tingly knowing that Liam carves out time to support his friend's kids.

"Great! We lost."

I stared at him, a little shocked. Surely I heard him wrong. No one should be happy their kid lost. "And that's great?"

"Yeah," he says with a laugh. "Because that means the season is over. You have no idea how insane the practices are." He puffs his cheeks and lets out a loud breath, emphasizing that it's a lot. And then he looks at me curiously. "Didn't Liam tell you you're on the VIP list? Next time, just come straight to the front. You don't need to wait."

"Must have slipped his mind," I said while my sisters audibly gasped. Ralph stepped aside to let us in and I touched his arm as I passed. "Thanks, Ralph."

"Shut up! VIP?" Autumn blurted, grabbing my hand as we made our way through the door. "Holly! Since when do you have bar pull? Who are you, and what have you done with my sister?"

"It's nothing," I muttered, feeling my face heat up. Thankfully, it was dark and crowded, so my sisters didn't notice. "Let's get a drink."

Dahlia led us to the bar, weaving through the crowd like she owned the place only to abandon us with, "I have to pee. Order me a seltzer beer. I'll find you in a minute."

I nodded absently and scanned the bar. My heart thudded as I searched for Liam. He was working a double this weekend, although he said that his shifts were different from everyone else's. He floated where needed. So, he could be making drinks, or bussing tables, or even kicking people out.

It took a painful minute, but then I saw him. He was at the far end of the bar closest to the dance floor, laughing at something a customer said as he filled a mug with the perfect balance of beer and foam. He looked radiant, completely in his element, exuding confidence. Liam was handsome this morning, but seeing him work the bar was sexy. Before I could stop myself, I was crossing the room and standing right in front of him.

When he saw me, his face lit up. "Holly! Twice in one day. How lucky am I?"

I swallowed hard, trying to keep my voice steady but the word *soulmate* kept flashing before my eyes in bright gold letters. I felt like I was going to puke, cry, and pass out all at once. But I didn't want Liam to know I was freaking out. So, I put on my best smile and said, "Maybe I'm the lucky one."

Liam leaned forward, resting his hands on the bar, his eyes locked on mine. There was an intensity in the way he looked at me. It drowned out everyone and everything around us. A girl could get used to a guy looking at her like this.

"What brings you in tonight?"

I hesitated, wondering if I should come up with some excuse, but clearly, I still had some alcohol in my veins because the truth slipped out before I could think of something smart to say. "I wanted to see you."

His grin softened into something warmer, something that

sent my stomach flipping in the best way. "I'm glad you did. Is it lame to say I missed you? I've been so busy I haven't had time to talk since breakfast. We had two bartenders and a busboy call out tonight. Thank God it's Sunday. We'd be dying if this were last night."

Before I could say anything else, Autumn's voice cut through the moment. "Holly!"

I turned to see her pushing through the crowd. "What are you doing? I was ordering drinks, and then you disappeared. You can't do that to me! I nearly had a heart attack! I nearly..." She looked past me to Liam and said, "Oh! Hi. Who are you?"

"Autumn," I said, shooting her a warning look. "This is Liam. Liam, this is my sister."

"Liam?" She questioned, her eyes raking over his crisp white button-down and the way he'd rolled the sleeves up to his elbows. "Are you flirting with my sister, or are you on a first-name basis with all the pretty girls tonight?"

My jaw dropped. I was shocked. Mortified! I couldn't tell if Autumn was trying to size Liam up or see if she had a chance with him. I didn't know whether to laugh off the comment or scold her. I didn't get a chance to do either because my other sisters decided to join us.

"Found them!" River shouted, and a second later, she and Dahlia were beside us. They both had drinks and when River noticed me looking at her hands, she added, "If you wanted a drink, then you shouldn't have run off."

And now we could add public scolding next to humiliation on the checklist for tonight. And here the adventure had started so well.

"Ignore them," I said playfully, but really, I was begging both Liam and the universe to listen. "In fact, ignore all three of my sisters because they are evil judgey sprites."

Dahlia arched her eyebrows, trying her best to give the warning look Mom used to do when one of us took things a step too far. I ignored her because, in my opinion, they had gone too far! Bringing my sisters out semi-drunk to unintentionally meet my potential soulmate might have been the worst mistake I'd made this decade.

Liam gave Autumn one of his easy, disarming smiles and handled the insult with ease. "It's safe to say the regulars know my name, but I don't give it out to just anyone." He reached for a glass and effortlessly filled it with ice as he said, "It's nice to meet you all."

"How do you know Holly?" River asked.

"The short answer is, we met at a bar." Liam turned and grabbed two bottles off the shelf behind him and filled a shot glass, then emptied the liquor into the cup. He added a dash of grenadine and then filled the cup with fruit juice. He then topped it with an orange slice and handed it to me. "Here. Can't have you being the odd one out."

"Oh. Thank you." I dug in my purse for my debit card, which had buried itself somewhere beside my wallet, three pens, a condom—that magically found its way into my purse, likely due to a little minx named Dahlia—and a half-eaten snack-sized bag of Cheetos. "I'll start a tab."

"Your drinks are on me tonight," Liam said, refusing my card. "Theirs too, if they're nice to you."

"Well, aren't you sweet?" Autumn leaned on the bar. Her gaze noticeably dropped to his ring finger. "And single?"

"Currently in an unofficially exclusive, complicated entanglement." He winked at me and I felt like I could die. Seriously. I'd rather the floor open up and suck me into the Otherworld than live through this moment.

Autumn stared at Liam, confused, and said, "Oh." But then a moment passed where she looked at me and she figured out what he meant, and then shouted, "Oh! OMG! You mean with Holly. You and Holly!"

If I could have run away and hid, I would have. For anyone who didn't know, I had five levels of embarrassment. One was mildly embarrassed, like when I had food stuck in my teeth while running a meeting. I was okay because we had just finished eating but it was still embarrassing. Level two was a hair worse. It was the type of embarrassment where you cringe a little harder, but it's manageable and usually laughable later. Forgetting someone's name mid-conversation and awkwardly trying to avoid admitting it would classify as a two.

Level three was noticeably uncomfortable, like when you laughed too loudly at a joke that wasn't that funny and realized everyone was staring at you. A level four was legitimately mortified, like the time I accidentally hit "reply all" on an email that was only meant for one person and filled with painfully personal information. And then, finally, there was a level five. Five was full-on humiliation. The kind of embarrassment that made you want to change your name and move to another country.

I was currently at level three-point-five and creeping toward a four. But Dahlia kept me rooted in my spot by throwing her arms around my shoulder and whispering, "You're glowing. Don't run from this."

She knows me too well.

I squeezed her arm and then took a sip of my drink. It was like a tropical paradise in my mouth. The perfect balance of sweet and sultry with no hint of liquor. Too many of these, and I'd be in trouble.

Without warning, River perked up at the opening cords carrying over the noise of the bar and shouted, "I love this song!"

She grabbed my hand and dragged me toward the dance floor, our sisters in tow. I looked over my shoulder apologetically, but Liam just grinned and waved me off. I watched him go back to working the bar for as long as I could until, eventually, there were too many bodies between us. And then, my sisters and I danced like we were still in my living room and no one was watching.

The night flew by in a blur. My sisters and I had been dancing for what felt like hours, our laughter echoing louder than the music. At some point, the heat of the dance floor became too much, and I leaned into River's ear. "I need another drink," I said, fanning myself dramatically.

"Don't take too long!" she called back, spinning toward Autumn as they got lost in the rhythm of the song.

I meandered my way back to the bar, taking my time as I tried to cool down. But when I reached the counter, I didn't order anything right away. Instead, I lingered, my fingers brushing the worn edge as I let my eyes wander back to Liam.

He was moving with practiced ease, pouring drinks and flashing a casual smile that seemed to make everyone around him feel like they belonged. But it wasn't until his gaze caught mine that my breath hitched. He smiled—not the one he gave his customers, but something softer, warmer, like it was meant just for me.

I stayed at that spot longer than I meant to, sipping my drink and stealing glances in his direction. Every time our eyes met, my stomach flipped.

A little while later, Liam crossed the bar toward me, his steps slow and deliberate. He leaned on the counter, his piercing eyes never leaving mine. "Are you Enjoying yourself?"

"More than I thought I would," I admitted, the honesty surprising me. I set my drink down and decided I needed water for the rest of the night. Being this open and honest was dangerous.

"Good. I'm glad." Liam extended his hand, palm up. "Would you like to dance?"

"Aren't you supposed to be working?"

Liam rounded the edge of the bar and then held his hand out to me again. "I'm friends with the boss. He won't care."

I hesitated, then slipped my hand into his and let him lead me onto the dance floor. His fingers curled around mine, and when he pulled me close, the rest of the room seemed to disappear. Liam held me close, slow stepping to a song that was made for bumping and grinding. I didn't care. I was just happy to be in his arms.

"You look happy," he murmured, that low rumble sending shivers down my spine.

"Funny enough, I am." I looked up into his eyes and the space between us grew charged with the kind of electricity that made it hard to think clearly. I didn't overthink. I just leaned in.

Liam met me halfway and pressed his lips to mine.

The kiss was soft at first, testing, but it quickly deepened, stealing my breath and grounding me all at once. His hand tightened slightly on my waist as if to keep me close and in that moment it was just him and I. No bar. No bet. Just us. I could have stayed there forever, floating in his arms, but the overhead lights flickered, signaling last call. Liam pulled away first but he didn't let me go.

I blinked, momentarily disoriented, as the noise and bustle of the bar came rushing back. Though as the world came into focus I noticed Liam's gaze stayed on me, steady and unwavering.

"That was..." he whispered, and I would have done anything for him to always look at me the way he was right then. He kissed the tip of my nose once before my sisters butted in and ruined the moment.

"Are you ready to head out?" Autumn called from behind me.

I spun in Liam's arms and rested against his chest. Our hearts raced in synchronized rhythms, singing the same song. I looked up at him right as he looked down at me and said, "I think I'll stay."

Chapter 10

HOLLY

In less than ten minutes, Ralph had escorted every wayward soul out of Abbott's and to their cars or into a taxi if he felt they couldn't safely drive. After thirty minutes, it was just him, Liam and I. Everyone else had finished their post shift cleanup and left.

Liam lingered, wiping down a table. The damp cloth caught the stickiness of spilled drinks and the chaos from earlier. He worked with a steady rhythm, quick but efficient.

"You're awfully quiet." My voice carried effortlessly across the room without the chatter and music I'd grown used to tonight. "I feel like I should have heard one of your lame dad jokes by now."

Liam tossed his rag into a bucket and crossed the room toward me, a playful grin lifting his lips. "They aren't lame."

I raised an eyebrow and folded my arms across my chest. Liam's jokes *were* lame, but I loved them. I looked forward to the random message once, sometimes twice, a day because it showed he was thinking about me. It made me feel less guilty about how often I thought about him. "Oh, please."

Liam leaned against the counter beside me. "I was saving my best material for the grand finale."

"Alright, then. Hit me with your best shot. Let's hear this so-called *grand finale*."

Liam inched closer and whispered like he was about to share a world-shattering secret. "What do you call a fake noodle?"

"A fake noodle?" I frowned, unable to figure out where he was going with this one. Sometimes I got the answers and stole his thunder, but this time I had no clue. "What?"

"An impasta," he said with a completely serious expression before flashing me that beautifully disarming smile.

I groaned so loudly it echoed through the empty bar. "That was so bad it actually hurt." I pressed a hand to my chest, trying not to smile. "Like, physically painful."

"Come on, that's comedy gold!"

"Gold, alright—fool's gold," I shot back, shaking my head but unable to suppress the laugh bubbling up.

Liam shrugged, unbothered, his grin as infuriatingly charming as ever. "Hey, you asked for my best. If you can't handle the classics, that's on you."

"Classics," I muttered, rolling my eyes, but my smile lingered. I shifted closer, eager to close the space between us. Ever since that dance, I've wanted his hands on me again and it's been damn near excruciating waiting for everyone to leave. One more person. All I needed was to wait out Ralph and I wouldn't have to worry about what anyone might see or hear tonight. "Where do you even learn jokes that bad?"

"My mom," Liam said, his voice so low it was almost a whisper. "She used to wake me up with one every morning before school."

The smile on my face faltered as his words sank in. He'd mentioned once, in passing, that she'd died when he was a kid. I didn't know what to say then, and I really didn't know what to say now. His grief was quiet, a dull ache that settled deep— different from the raw wound of losing my mom last year, but just as familiar. I wondered if he clung to the little details like I did: the sound of her voice, the way she smiled. Or had time blurred those memories into something bittersweet?

Before I could respond, Ralph poked his head out, jangling

his keys. The tense moment shattered like glass and I couldn't have been more grateful for the change. "You two good here? Want me to wait, or are you locking up?"

"I've got it," Liam said, waving him off. "Have a good night."

Ralph's gaze flicked between us, a knowing look in his eyes. "Alright. Don't stay too late. And set the alarm this time." He didn't wait for Liam's rebuttal before scurrying out the door. I wanted to think he left so quickly because he was tired, but I had a feeling he knew what I had planned and wanted no part of it.

As the back door clicked shut behind him, the room felt even quieter. I leaned against the bar's edge, my arms crossed as I looked around. "It's weird seeing this place empty," I said nervously. "So different. Almost... romantic."

The word hung in the air between us for a long moment. Liam's finger brushed against my forearm. I looked down at it and then up at him. His eyes fixed on my lips, the dark of his pupils swallowing his sapphire eyes.

"Would I be a terrible friend," he asked, his voice low, "if I said I wanted to kiss you again?"

My heart skipped. I tilted my head, letting a slow smile spread across my lips. "I'd say you'd be a *great* friend if you did."

Liam's hand brushed the side of my face as he leaned in. He angled his head and pressed his mouth to mine. Unlike the first two, this kiss was slower, deliberate. I slid my hands up his arms, gripping the fabric of his shirt as I leaned into him. His hands traveled under my shirt, up my back and unclasped my bra. I pulled back just long enough to slip the fabric over my head and let my bra fall to the floor. Liam's shirt was off just as fast. His hands were back at my hips, grabbing me by the belt loops and pulling me onto his lap.

He kissed me again and my hips had a mind of their own. I was grinding against his lap, panting against his lips, and feeling like I'd die if we didn't take things to the next step.

"Is there a chance anyone could come back tonight?" I asked.

I wasn't shy, but I didn't want to be interrupted. We'd barely gotten to do anything fun, just kissing and grinding, and I was already chasing the next high that came from his touch.

"I'll fire them if they do," he said, his lips tracing down my neck to my collarbone. I made a sound that was somewhere between a sigh and a moan, and Liam grunted in return.

The things he did to me felt amazing, better than amazing, but it wasn't enough. I needed more than just his chest pressed to mine. I needed to feel him, every inch of the hardness pressing against me through his pants, and this stupid stool we'd found ourselves on wasn't suitable for the things I wanted to do.

Liam somehow read my mind because his hands slid under my thighs. He stood and muttered, "I've got you," while carrying us away from the bar. He took me to the break room and if I had any sort of conscience, I'd have felt terrible knowing that a kid slept here from time to time. But I didn't. I didn't think about anything beyond the burning desire to feel him.

He lowered me onto the cushions so we could both move like we wanted to. He settled between my legs, feverishly pulling my jeans and panties off my hips until he had me how he wanted me. Naked. Sitting on his face. His tongue brushed against my clit and I made embarrassing, gasping sounds that were a mix of Liam and God's name. He chuckled and the vibration was heavenly. I grasped at the cushions, his hair, his back. Anything to help bring me back to earth because I could have sworn I was floating outside my body. My thighs shook and a liquid heat swelled in my center.

Liam gripped my hips tighter. "I can't wait to taste you."

That, right there, sent me over the edge into the best third-base orgasm I'd ever experienced. It ripped through me, crackling like fire until all I could see was gold sparkles around the room. I was high on Liam's touch, every nerve in my body alive and aching for more when a strange vibration deep inside me broke through the haze. I had felt it earlier, a subtle thrum when

Liam first went down on me, but I had brushed it off, thinking it was just the effects of his touch.

Liam wiped his mouth with the back of his hand, his eyes dark and full of heat as he crawled up my body. His lips found mine and I loved how he tasted like me. I melted into him, desperate for more—to finally feel the bulge beneath his pants. But the vibration grew stronger. It pulled me out of the moment and tugged at the edge of my awareness like a relentless whisper.

His fingers threaded through my hair, sending shivers down my spine. And then it hit me—what that feeling was.

Magic.

It surged between us, wrapping around our bodies in golden threads, a living thing that pulsed with hunger, waiting for us to connect, to bind our souls together. My breath caught in my throat at the realization of what was happening.

Dahlia had been right all along.

Liam was my soulmate.

Panic surged through me, sharp and suffocating. I jerked back, breaking the kiss as the words tumbled out of me. "I'm sorry. I have to go."

Liam recoiled, confusion and hurt flashing across his face as he sat back on his heels. "Did I do something wrong?" His voice was low, almost a whisper. The rawness in it cut through me, but I had to ignore it.

"No," I blurted, fumbling to pull my pants back on. My hands trembled as I searched for my shoes. How had they come off? And when? I had no idea, but I was grateful they were at the edge of the couch. "I just... I can't do this. I'm sorry. I... just..."

My words dissolved into nothing as I stumbled into the main room of the bar. I yanked my shirt over my head and clutched my bra in one hand, not bothering to put it on. My magic writhed inside me, a living force straining against my control. It pulsed and ached, the golden threads desperate to weave themselves tighter, to complete the bond it knew we both wanted. It burned with longing, a yearning that mirrored my own, and it tore me apart because I couldn't give in. I *shouldn't* give in.

The door behind me opened, and Liam stepped out, his expression crumbling the moment our eyes met. The open vulnerability on his face made my heart splinter. He looked shattered—broken in a way I had never seen anyone suffer before. "Can I drive you home?"

The gentleness in his voice hurt more than if he'd been angry.

"No, Liam," I said, harsher than I intended. He flinched, and I bit my lip, guilt pooling in my chest. "Just... just let me go."

For a moment, he stared at me, his jaw tight, his eyes filled with questions he didn't ask. Then, slowly, he nodded. "Okay."

And he let me go.

Each step away from him felt like a blade slicing through my heart. I had told him to let me leave, and he had listened—just as I'd wanted. But a huge part of me wished he hadn't. Wished he had fought for me. Wished he had pulled me back into his arms and refused to let go.

Because as much as my magic burned and as terrifying as this bond was... I wanted him.

Chapter 11

LIAM

I couldn't sleep. I laid there for hours, staring at the ceiling fan as it spun in slow, hypnotic circles. The faint hum of the motor filled the silence, a small distraction from the thoughts I couldn't escape while dim light filtered through the curtains, painting the walls of my bedroom in muted shades of gray. I hadn't even bothered to change when I got home. Holly's perfume clung to my shirt like a ghost I wasn't ready to part with. It was floral but not overpowering, subtle yet unforgettable —just like her.

I wanted to believe everything was fine. That her leaving so abruptly this morning was nothing. We'd had a moment—one I'd wanted so badly, for so long—and yet, somehow, it had slipped through my fingers.

Again.

I sat up slowly, feeling the weight of the night settle deeper into my chest. I ran a hand through my hair, gripping it lightly at the roots as if that could ground me. There was an ache inside me I didn't know what to do with, a hollow thrum where my heart should've been. It was like my soul had split in two.

A part of me had seen this coming. Holly had run from me before. Why should this time have been any different? People didn't change. It's a fact I've told myself countless times, but even as I thought it, something inside me protested.

People could change.

Life forced you to, whether you wanted it or not. Every decision, every yes or no, every ignored text or answered call shaped you into someone new. I wanted to believe that. Needed to believe it, because if it wasn't true, then I was a fool.

I exhaled sharply, the sound breaking the stillness of the room. I stood and moved through the condo, my steps heavy against the hardwood floor. I grabbed my phone off the coffee table and stared at it, my thumb hovering over her name in my contacts. Holly had left so quickly. Something spooked her. I should've given her space. I should've given my pride a chance to heal. But I couldn't stand this half-empty feeling anymore.

I pressed the call button before I could second-guess myself.

It rang once, then it went to voicemail.

Hey, it's Holly! Leave a message and I'll call you back.

Her voice—bright, effortless, full of life—twisted the knife that already lodged itself in my chest. My throat tightened. I couldn't bring myself to leave a message. Instead, I stared at the screen until the call disconnected and the home screen stared back at me.

She ignored me.

If the call hadn't gone through at all, I could've convinced myself her phone was dead or turned off. But to ignore me... That hurt more than I wanted to admit. I sank onto the couch, the ache in my chest sharpening with every passing second.

Last night felt so real. She'd been there, in my arms, looking at me like she finally wanted the same thing I did. Like she was ready to give us a chance.

God, I'd thought this time was different.

I glanced at the clock—7 a.m. Maybe it was too early. Maybe she had a full day ahead of her, meetings or deadlines she couldn't ignore. That had to be it. She just needed space.

But even as I tried to rationalize it, I couldn't stop myself. I opened my messages and typed out a quick text.

Morning. Everything okay?

I hit send and set the phone down, watching it like it might grow legs and run. The seconds dragged into minutes, then stretched into an hour. Still nothing. I paced the living room, my movements restless and aimless. Stopping at the window, I looked down at the street below. The city was waking up. People bustled to work, taxis honked impatiently, and life carried on as if my entire world hadn't just been turned upside down.

By lunchtime, I couldn't take it anymore. I sent another message.

Do you want to grab dinner tonight?

I didn't expect an answer—not right away—but a part of me clung to the hope that she'd reply eventually. Hours passed. The sun dipped lower in the sky, casting long shadows across the room. The silence from my phone felt deafening.

It was almost eight by the time I gave up staring at the screen. I leaned against the window, defeated, and pressed my forehead to the cool glass. The faint trace of Holly's perfume still lingered on my shirt, cruel and comforting all at once.

I sank back onto the couch, exhaustion pulling at me, but I couldn't let go of yesterday. Not yet. Maybe it was ridiculous. Maybe I was just fooling myself. But there was this irrational part of me that believed if I held on a little longer, if I waited just a bit more, she'd come back.

But as the hours dragged into the night, a heavier thought settled over me, suffocating and inescapable.

Maybe last night was all I'd get.

Maybe running into her on St. Patrick's Day wasn't fate giving us another chance.

Maybe it was just a cruel coincidence.

And maybe—just maybe—it was time to stop chasing someone who didn't want to be caught.

Chapter 12

Three nights later, four of my employees and I gathered in my kitchen. I could feel their eyes on me, each gaze a mixture of expectation, worry, and curiosity. I'd never called a meeting like this before. It had always been the whole team or me and the managers. Not this hodgepodge mix of two bartenders, a bouncer, and a line cook. And never at my house.

Amber leaned forward, her dark hair slipping over one shoulder as she traced the rim of her glass absentmindedly. Ralph sat beside her tapping a steady, rhythmic beat that highlighted his impatience. Cam leaned back in my living room chair, arms crossed, his ever-present smirk masking whatever he was really thinking and, across from him, Mara watched me closely, waiting for me to start the meeting.

I took a deep breath and tried to ignore the heaviness that wore on me like an oversized coat. The ache of Holly's rejection was still raw and painful. I had hoped the feeling would ease overtime, but each day the suffocating sensation only got worse. I knew how I sounded. We weren't anything serious—friends with the prospect of more—but the hole she left in me was as deep as the ones left by every girl who'd broken my heart before her. Possibly worse. The pain made no sense, but it didn't matter. Logic rarely played a role in heartbreak.

"There's no way I can save Abbott's," I started. Each word felt like a bitter confession as it left my lips. At this point, I'd be wasting my time trying to win the bet because the only person I wanted to be with didn't want me. I was a mess emotionally—and judging by the way Amber had wrinkled her nose at me... twice—I looked just as bad as I felt. I caught my reflection in the window: rumpled clothes, shadows under my eyes, and the unmistakable weariness of someone who'd lost too many hours of sleep. I looked like the ghost of the man I used to be, a sorry consolation prize for any wife, even if she were only in it for the money.

Silence hung heavy in the room. My friends stared back at me with the same haunting expression I'd run from my whole life. Disappointment.

"But," I continued, meeting their eyes one by one, "I can start something new. People don't love Abbott's because of the games or the decor. They love it because of us—what we've built."

"And the location," Cam muttered, earning a sharp *shhh* from Mara. He was a ball-buster with good intentions—usually. Today, though, he just wanted to poke the bear, and I wasn't biting.

"We can find another spot." My grip tightened around the edge of the counter. I needed them to believe in my plan. Together we could do this. Was Abbott's in a prime part of town? Yes, but location was second to the people who brought the place to life. Without my team, I'd fail in the first year. "A *better* spot."

Amber tilted her head, her expression softening as her dark eyes searched mine. "What happened with Holly?" she asked quietly. "You two seemed to really hit it off."

"I thought so too," I admitted, the raw truth scraping out of me. "But even if we were to have made things work, she was never going to marry me. Which is why I started on plan B last week."

Amber nodded slowly, her gaze understanding but not prying. She didn't push and I was grateful for it.

"What do you say?" I asked, meeting each of their eyes in turn. "Are you in this with me?"

Ralph leaned forward, his earlier impatience gone. His face was serious now, all traces of jest wiped clean by the gravity of the moment. "What do you need from us, boss?"

I looked at him, then at the others. "Time," I said simply, "and a place."

The sharp *slap* of a palm hitting the bar jolted me out of my spiraling thoughts. I blinked, startled, and looked up to see Cam grinning. His eyes sparkled with mischief, the kind that danced dangerously close to madness, but behind it all, there was pride —pure, unfiltered pride—like he'd just unearthed the answer to every problem we'd ever faced.

"What's this?" I asked as he shoved a crumpled packet of paper toward me.

"This," he declared, leaning forward with the kind of theatrical flair that could've sold snake oil, "is where we make *Abbott's 2.0.*"

I unfolded the paper, my brow furrowing as I took in the advertisement for a building; floor plans, rough sketches of what I think was supposed to be a restaurant, and a handful of grainy photos.

"It's an inn," I said flatly.

Cam's grin didn't falter. He snatched the pages and flipped through the packet with a dramatic flourish. "*No,*" he corrected, tapping an image with triumph. "It's a *beachside* inn and restaurant. And it's *cheap.* Technically, it's in Ponte Vedra, but it's only a fifteen-minute drive from here."

I squinted at the faded images—peeling paint, cracked tile, sagging railings. "Cam, this place is falling apart and Inns come with restrictions and codes we've never dealt with before."

It was like I hadn't even spoken. Cam flipped to another page and countered, "It doesn't *have* to be an inn. We can renovate the suites upstairs—there are twelve of them—and make you a three or four bedroom condo."

I lifted a brow. "I *have* a condo."

He waved me off like I was missing the point. "Sell it. Rent it out. Who cares? Because *this*—" he jabbed the page hard enough to crinkle it, "—is a goldmine."

The words hung in the air, too bold, too brash, but something in them tugged at me. I sighed, my mind churning with what-ifs and half-formed plans. "Say we renovate six suites and build me a killer home, what about the rest?"

Cam's grin stretched wider, practically daring me to dream bigger. "We combine singles into two-bedroom apartments. Fair warning, I'm moving into one."

I scoffed. "Oh, you are?"

"Hell, yeah! And if we combine these two over here," he said, pointing to a corner of the floor plan, "Amber could move in too. It would give her a place to work and somewhere her kid can be safe while she does."

I glanced at Amber across the bar. She shrugged, a slow smile tugging at the corners of her mouth, and I realized Cam had already gone to her first. Possibly the others, too.

"You've really thought this through," I murmured, a thread of admiration slipping into my voice.

"Damn right I have." He nudged the paper closer. "Look at the price."

I did, and my jaw clenched. It was cheap—*too* cheap. "It needs work."

"It *does*," Cam admitted, his grin undeterred. "But my brother's construction company can knock it out in no time."

"How much time is 'no time'?"

"Six months tops," he said confidently, as if it were already a done deal.

"I have three." A little less if he were counting, but rounding up sounded easier than saying two months, three weeks, and four days.

Cam shrugged, unfazed by my ticking timeline. "Do you want it done or done *right?*"

I turned to Amber, who'd been watching me, reading my reactions. I needed her to be my bar manager on this one. She needed to love the location, but even more so if she were to live there. "What do you think?"

After a long moment, Amber said, "I think that if we're doing this, we need to do it right. It's not just a fresh start for you, but for all of us. And…" She swallowed hard. "If you're open to the idea, we threw around the possibility of being partners. I couldn't afford to contribute much, but I'd finally have something that would be mine."

I looked down at the pictures again and tried to imagine what Abbott's 2.0 would look like. How we would renovate the halls to ensure Stephanie's safety without the building feeling like a cage. And what would a real partnership with people who respected my opinions be like?

"Partners means you wouldn't have to worry about us bailing," Ralph added. "And we don't want much, five percent each, because we can't help with much financially, but we'll put our blood, sweat, and tears into this place if you let us."

I looked at each of them, my heart pounding with a determination that burned hotter with every second. They wanted this, possibly even more than I did. "Mara's on board too?"

"Yes!" her voice said, carrying through the fabric of Cam's front pocket shirt. He pulled out his phone and shrugged.

I laughed for the first time in days. The Inn needed so much work, but Cam's brother was a contractor with a great reputation. He would get the job done. If my team could keep this bar functioning in my absence, I could cover everything monetarily. The plan was crazy and half-cocked, but I loved it.

"Okay, team. Let's make it happen."

Chapter 13

HOLLY

I was a coward.

It wasn't easy to admit, but the truth sat heavy in my chest as I refreshed Liam's Instagram page for the third time today. His posts hadn't changed all week—just the same blurry photo of Cam, his line cook, flipping burgers behind the bar grill, and a close-up of a perfectly poured tequila with an orange slice on the glass's rim, paired with a caption that made me ache: *Missing something today, but the show goes on.*

The comments were playful, filled with inside jokes from regulars and a handful of strangers saying they'd order one tonight... even though for some of those people their tonight was three nights ago. But no one knew what I knew—Liam posted that for me. Possibly as an olive branch since I'd ignored every call and text he'd sent. What started as a flood of communication on day one had trickled into a single text every day or so. I knew they'd stop altogether if I didn't do something soon.

The potential abandonment hurt in ways I didn't know were possible. It had been two weeks since I ran and the ache of leaving hadn't dulled. It wasn't just guilt—it was something else. Something primal. Something terrifying.

Our bond.

The ugly truth that we were soulmates.

Even thinking the word made my heart race in an *I might puke then pass out* sort of way. The idea of one person being destined for me should've felt romantic. Magical even. But it was suffocating. To love someone so deeply meant giving them the power to destroy you. I never wanted someone to have that kind of control over me. I wanted love, but I wanted the freedom to walk away if we grew apart. I wasn't sure that was possible for us because my magic complicated things.

Still, ignoring Liam was probably the hardest thing I'd ever done, which was why I'd blocked his number and deleted it from my phone. The temptation to call him was too strong.

But that didn't mean I couldn't low-key creep on him.

I swiped the screen and switched from his personal account to Abbott's business page. Liam had updated the hours and made a post about exciting changes on the horizon. Nothing specific about the bet, but knowing him, he was probably working on plan B—a new Abbott's. Guilt rocked me to my core. I said I'd help him get things off the ground and here I was hiding. I was a terrible person.

A knock on my door startled me out of my guilt-ridden thoughts. Every instinct warned me to ignore it. Liam hadn't popped by yet, which was surprising considering how our friendship started. He was so determined to be a part of my life that I half expected him to show up the day after I ran and demand an explanation. He never came. It didn't mean he still couldn't or that I was ready to face him if he were at the door, but I just thought... I sighed. I didn't know what I thought. Or wanted.

"Holly, open up," Dahlia's voice called from outside. "I've got pizza and wine, and I'm not leaving until you let me in."

A strange feeling shot through me. I was both relieved and disappointed she wasn't Liam. I teasingly groaned loud enough for her to hear, got up, and opened the door. Dahlia breezed past me, balancing a pizza box in one hand and holding a bottle of wine in the other. She went straight to the living room, set them on the coffee table, then proceeded to scold me. "You've been ghosting everyone for almost two weeks now. What the hell is going on?"

"Nothing," I muttered, crossing my arms. This wasn't Dahlia's job. I was the mother hen of the group. I kept everyone's life on track, not her. My track may be a little messy right now, but everything that mattered was still moving forward. She didn't need to come and do... whatever this was.

"Right." Dahlia walked into my kitchen and grabbed two glasses. She then popped the cork on the wine and poured. "Care to explain why you've been ignoring everyone? And don't give me some bullshit excuse about work."

I took the outstretched glass and sank onto the couch. The move was risky, but my dark cushions had hidden more than one accidental spill over the years. I stared at the hazy pink liquid like it held the answers to my problems. For anyone wondering, it did not. I tried soul-searching in a bottle of wine twice now and discovered that I had turned into the kind of girl who may or may not have driven past Abbott's to see if Liam's car was in the parking lot.

"I needed time to think."

"Think about what?" Dahlia grabbed a slice of pizza and sat next to me. She chewed on a cheesy bite, casually waiting for me to bare my soul.

I hesitated. Dahlia might've been my sister and closest friend, but this? This was too raw, too personal.

"Liam," she said after finishing nearly half her slice while waiting for me to answer. She tossed what was left on the cardboard box and leveled her gaze on me. "This is about Liam, isn't it?"

My heart skipped a beat. Was I that transparent? I didn't think I looked heartbroken. I'd showered, shaved, and even made a point to style my hair. I didn't have much experience with broken hearts, but every time Autumn got dumped she looked like hell. Matted hair, blotchy skin. The same sweatpants and t-shirt for days. Plus, the baking. We'd have to intervene and take all of her flour and sugar away, or else she'd gain ten pounds.

I thought I looked fine. Because I was fine. I traded my wine for pizza and shot Dahlia a look that said *see, I'm fine,* but stupidly said, "I don't want to talk about Liam."

Dahlia narrowed her eyes but didn't press. Instead, she picked up her slice of pizza and chewed thoughtfully. After a moment, she said, "I met him, you know. At the bar on St. Patrick's Day."

My head snapped up. "You what?"

Anger burned a hole through my haze of heartbreak. Dahlia swore, over and over again, that she didn't use her magic on me. She insisted that I wasn't under one of her love spells gone wrong. And now she admitted that she lied! I could've killed her. Hell, if her mismatched lovers felt this terrible when their love spells didn't work out, they probably wanted to kill her, too! Well, they would've if they knew what she did to them.

"Relax," she said, holding up a hand. "I didn't influence him or anything. We just talked."

My stomach twisted as my thoughts spiraled back to that first night. I knew something felt off between us, but I think I hoped our connection was real and I was just scared. "Talked about what?"

"Him, mostly." She leaned back, swirling her wine. "I don't think I've ever explained but with my magic, the world is a sea of colors. People's auras don't light up until they're near their soulmates. That's how I know who to pair together. That night, Liam lit up gold. It confused me because no one else matched his spirit."

Gold. Like the threads of magic that wrapped around us. I stared at her, my heart pounding. Hoping. Fearing. Wanting...

"Then, he asked about you," Dahlia continued, her gaze steady. "And I had a hunch. One that was confirmed during our last girls' night. When I saw you light up gold, too."

I reached for my glass of wine and nearly spilled it because my hands were trembling so badly.

"Holly," Dahlia said softly, leaning forward. She took the glass from me and set it on the table, then held my hand. "I didn't meddle in your love life. I never have, and I never will. But you're being a fool if you let Liam go. He's the one you've been waiting for."

Tears burned my eyes. I bit down hard on my lip, hoping the sting would hold them back, but all it did was send the flood spilling over. "What happens if I don't accept the bond? Will he be lonely for the rest of his life?"

"No," Dahlia said, shaking her head. "He'll be broken for a while, but eventually, his soul will split. One piece will always belong to you, but it will search for another rejected bond to match with." She hesitated, the truth pressing heavy between us. "But it will *never* be the same. It will never feel as right as it could have with you."

My breath hitched as the ache in my chest grew unbearable. *He'll move on.* The thought was supposed to be comforting, but it only hollowed me out. I squeezed my eyes shut, as if that could block out the truth.

"I..." I looked at her again. "I don't want to hurt him. I don't want to break him."

"Then don't," she whispered.

But fear had already taken root, its thorny vines tangling in my heart. I didn't want to ask the next question. Didn't want to give voice to the terror that gripped me, but it tore free, raw and desperate.

"What if you're wrong?" My voice cracked. "What if I start a life with Liam—build something real—and then in March..." My breath caught as a sob hitched in my throat. "What if my magic stirs? What if Mom was wrong? What if there's no escaping this curse, no running from this life?"

"Holly," Dahlia said firmly, her eyes blazing with determination. "You can't live your life in a world of 'what ifs.' You have to decide what you want and say, 'fuck the consequences.' You'll never find happiness if you live in that grey area. It all comes down to, what do you want?"

I stared at her, my heart in my throat. What did I want? For the first time since my magic stirred to life, I let myself imagine what it would be like to settle down. To be with Liam.

I took a deep breath, already knowing the answer and hoped I wasn't too late.

Chapter 14

HOLLY

By the time I finally mustered the courage to face Liam, three agonizing weeks had crawled by since I'd ghosted him. Two days since Dahlia's—for lack of better words —intervention. Every single day had been a battle—fighting with my heart, arguing with my head, and losing to both. But today... Today, I was done fighting. I was ready.

At least, that's what I told myself as I gripped Abbott's door handle, my fingers trembling so badly that I almost dropped my keys.

The familiar scent of hops and worn wood greeted me as I stepped inside, but something was off. It was still early—only six o'clock on a Friday—but the energy was different. Subdued. Muted. Patrons I assumed were regulars sat in their usual spots, nursing beers and murmuring to one another, but the electric hum of life that usually pulsed through the place was... dimmed. Maybe it was because the night was young. Or maybe it was because something was missing.

I swallowed hard, my heart thundering as I scanned the room.

Liam wasn't behind the bar.

He wasn't at any of the tables.

Could he have been in the back? Was he even here? Panic fluttered in my chest. *Why hadn't I checked for his car?* The nerves that had turned my stomach to knots in the parking lot had been so overwhelming that I'd barely noticed my own reflection in the rearview mirror, let alone thought to look for *him*.

"Holly!"

I jumped at the sound of my name.

Ralph came from the hallway that led to the lounge and office. I hadn't even noticed he wasn't out front at the door. Had he been watching for me? Waiting? Warning Liam I was here so he could run?

"Long time no see." His warm smile softened the sharp edges of my anxiety, but there was a flicker of curiosity in his eyes that made me squirm

"Yeah, hi." I forced a smile and shoved my hands into my pockets so he wouldn't see them tremble. "Uh... is Liam here?"

"Not today." Ralph shook his head, then added carefully, "He's over at the new spot. Renovations and all that. You should check it out."

He reached for a napkin, scrawled an address on it, and slid it across the bar. The ink smudged under my fingers as I picked up the paper-thin cloth.

"Thanks," I whispered, my voice barely audible.

Ralph's smile softened further and there was what looked like a flicker of relief in his eyes. "Go easy on him," he said quietly.

Easy on him? I was the one walking toward a guillotine. Liam did what he was supposed to. He made the effort, showed me I was still on his mind, hinted that he was still interested, and I gave him nothing except for a read receipt. I nodded, my throat too tight to speak, then headed out with the napkin clenched tightly in my hand.

This wasn't a bar.

It was an inn. A rundown, weather-beaten inn that looked as though it had been plucked straight from the eighties and then forgotten about. The building was a two-story structure with pale, sun-bleached pink paint and turquoise shutters. It had a large wooden deck that wrapped around its front, though it had seen better days. A few faded deck chairs sat abandoned on the wraparound porch, their cushions flattened and covered with a fine layer of dust or maybe sand.

I counted six workers bustling about, balancing sheets of plywood on their shoulders or hoisting stacks of materials into their arms. Ladders leaned precariously against the walls, and the rhythmic pounding of hammers echoed in the quiet evening air.

I double-checked the address scrawled on the napkin Ralph had given me, my thumb brushing over the numbers. Was this really the place? Liam's new venture? I sat there, trying to understand why he'd chosen something so... dilapidated.

The longer I sat in my car, the more I second-guessed everything. Maybe this was a mistake. Maybe he wouldn't want to see me. Maybe—

A sharp knock on my window made me jump.

I turned, startled, to see a man wearing a yellow hard hat with a dust-covered bandana pulled over his mouth. His eyes squinted with curiosity and, after a moment, he tugged the bandana down to reveal a friendly, slightly familiar looking grin.

"Can I help you?" He shouted.

I rolled down the window, heart hammering in my chest. There was no turning back now. Unless this was the wrong address, then I'd take the mixup as a sign from fate that Liam and I weren't meant to be. That Dahlia was wrong and...

And this guy was staring at me, still waiting for my answer.

"Uh... maybe. Is Liam here?"

He raised a brow, clearly amused, before widening his grin. "Yeah. I'll take you to him."

My hands shook as I grabbed my keys and climbed out of the car. There really was no turning back now. I followed the guy through a glass-paned door that had seen better days. The white paint had chipped away on nearly half of it and one of the glass panels was cracked.

"Boss! Got a surprise for you!" He shouted once we were deep inside the drywall dust-covered room. I looked around, trying to visualize Liam's plan. The space had promise. It had been gutted down to the studs—which would need a decorative flair—but overall, it was a large open room. Tables lined the center where it looked like Liam would build a large rectangular bar, and an additional bar was already built into the structure that serviced both the back of the room and the outside patio. Outside, I could see a large wooden deck that overlooked the ocean and a mostly, if not completely, empty pool.

The sound of heavy footsteps carried down a set of stairs and a muttered curse preceded a frustrated sigh. "Cam, I swear, if this is another one of your—"

Liam came into view, his gray T-shirt streaked with dust and jeans worn and frayed at the knees. His brow furrowed as he wiped a hand down his face, but he froze when his eyes locked on me. "Holly?"

The way he said my name—it wasn't just a word. It sounded like a prayer. A whispered, desperate hope.

Cam's grin widened as he turned to leave us alone. "I'll clear everyone out," he said right before yelling, "Time to call it a day, boys!"

The clamor of tools and the hum of conversation carried into the room, but I hardly noticed because all I could focus on was the sound of my racing heart and the way Liam was looking at me. He took a step closer, his eyes searching mine, as if he couldn't quite believe I was standing there.

"I..." A warm, fuzzy vibration stirred inside me. My magic was waking and it was long past March seventeenth, which meant Dahlia was right. There was no doubt that Liam was my soulmate. The pain of longing eased and for the first time in weeks, I felt like I was where I was meant to be. "I came to see you."

Liam's lips twitched, almost smiling, but his guard remained up. "It's been a while."

"I know," I whispered, closing the space between us. "And I'm sorry. I was scared. What I feel when I'm with you... it's overwhelming. I haven't been in a relationship since high school, and I wasn't sure I'd ever jump into one again."

His eyes softened, the tension in his shoulders easing just enough to show the cracks in his armor. He wanted this. *Please tell me he still wants this.* "And now?"

I took a shaky breath and swallowed hard. "Now, I'd like to try. To date you. If that's still on the table."

For a heartbeat, neither of us moved. I watched him, painstakingly waiting for him to split my soul in two and accept me. He didn't know what he was accepting, but on the surface of my lineage and the craziness this world calls love—though I'm not ready to give my feelings that label—I needed him to accept me. My flaws. My insecurities. My crazy sisters.

Me.

"Yeah, it is."

Liam's arms wrapped around me and my magic surged. It danced, flowing in happy waves and twisting into coils. I stayed there, breathing in the sweet scent of his musk. Taking in the hard curves of his body. I could have stayed there with him forever, but I wanted more than just a hug. I wanted to finish what we'd started back at Abbott's.

The moment I looked up at Liam, his hands cupped my cheeks and he dipped his head, lips pressing against mine. All the other times we kissed it felt like he was ravenous, feeding an insatiable hunger. This kiss was different. Slower. Like I was something precious to savor. It lasted for a minute, then two, then... Well, then I lost all concept of time.

I looped my arms around his neck, needing to touch more of him, and he lifted me off the ground. My legs wrapped around his waist as he carried me to one of the dusty work tables. He set me on it, then pushed the papers, pens, and haphazardly forgotten tools to the floor. I reach for his shirt and tug it overhead. Somehow, I'd forgotten how beautiful he was. His hard edges were tanned and toned but not beefy. A thin dusting of chest hair covered his pecs and funneled down his stomach, paving a taunting trail to the goods beneath his pants.

"I want this," Liam said, one arm on either side of me, caging me in. "But not if you're going to run again. We can take things as slow as you need. Whatever it takes to keep you here."

"I'm accepting our bond, Liam," I cupped his cheeks and looked him in the eyes. I needed him to know that I meant every word and I wasn't going anywhere.

"What?"

"Nothing," I said, shaking my head. I wasn't going to get into the details. It didn't matter. I was Liam's and my magic hummed with the anticipation of making it official. I kissed him and pulled him on top of me as I laid on the table. I reached for his zipper and struggled to get his pants off, but between my hands, my feet, and an uncoordinated shimmy, I finally had him how I wanted him. Well, almost. His boxers still stood between me and what I needed, but not for long.

I reached between the slit of his boxers and wrapped my fingers around his cock. I stroked his long, silky length, my fingertips far from touching. Liam's head dropped to my shoulder and he bit down. I sighed his name, "Liam," and he dipped his hand between my legs, pushing my pantie aside. I could have died right there and been happy. He played with my clit while I tried to make him feel just as good. But he was ruthless, pulling my arousal from me, bringing me to the edge of ecstasy, just to leave me wanting more.

"Holly," he panted, my name a plea on his lips as he broke our kiss. He wanted me just as much as I wanted him. I saw it in the way he looked at me. Felt it in the way his dick pulsed in my palm when he said my name. "I don't have a condom."

My magic wrapped around us, golden threads tangling and twisting, waiting with heated impatience. I squirmed beneath him, pressure building inside me as his thumb rubbed against my clit. "I'm on the pill," I said, nipping at his ear. "So long as you're clean, I trust you."

I hoped my magic wouldn't match me with someone who had a gross STD. I liked to think it was sensible and wouldn't give me a nasty surprise as its going away gift.

"I'm good. I promise," he said, slipping a finger inside me. I gasped, unable to take the sensation anymore, and came all over his hand.

"That's my good girl." Liam kissed the inside of my thigh and then sat back on his heels. He slid my panties off. Tossed them to the side. Spread my legs open. And positioned himself between them.

There was a breathless moment where he hesitated and I wondered if he had changed his mind. Liam might not have understood what us getting together meant, but maybe some part of him could sense how monumental this moment was. He stared into my eyes, the gold fleck in his greens glowing bright, and I was convinced this wasn't happening. But then he smiled and slowly pressed into me.

It should have been awkward, and perhaps with anyone else this level of intimacy would have been. I'd had my fair share of hookups over the years, and this first step was always rushed. A quick thrust and boom the fun began. Sometimes there was a slower start, but that usually had to do with me not being wet enough and friction. That wasn't the case with Liam. I was hot and wet and wanting and he... he was savoring the moment.

He sucked in an audible breath once he was in and stilled again.

"You okay?" I asked. I'd never felt so vulnerable. I wasn't used to this tenderness. The guys I hooked up with were the *wham, bam, thank you ma'am* sort. There was no thought or feeling beyond the race to finish. With Liam, there were butterflies, anticipation, a heightened sense of elatement with every touch. He could have sneezed on me and I probably would have felt the ghost's touch of an orgasm.

"Mmhmm." Liam kissed the tip of my nose and the movement of his body shifting made him grunt. "I'm just trying really hard not to come right now."

"We've got all night." I laughed a little and hooked my legs around his waist.

"No. I need you to come first." He bit down my shoulder and a zing of pleasure shot from my shoulder straight through me. My back arched. Liam moved not to lose me and I dissolved into a sticky pool of pleasure. With each thrust I lost myself in the way he made me feel. Beautiful. Desired. And oh so good. A distant part of me felt my magic tying us together but I was too lost in the next round of pleasure building to care.

Liam pinned my hands above my head and rutted into me. He thrusted deeper, and harder, until there was nothing I could do but scream his name. I came harder and more viscous than I ever had in my life. Liam's release was moments later, and as he pulled out and came on his shirt, my body was quiet. My magic had left me but in its place was a new sensation.

The feeling of being utterly and completely whole.

Epilogue

Saint Patrick's Day. One Year later

"What are you drinking?" the man across the bar asked. He wore large green overalls without a shirt and a top hat. He looked like most everyone tonight, dressed to celebrate their favorite drinking holiday in various shades of green.

It was strange, having that phrase catch my attention tonight instead of the one I'd heard for so many years. *Wanna get lucky?* But it was nice too.

Just like Mom promised, my magic left when Liam and I got together. It hadn't stirred or even fizzled all year, although that wasn't unexpected. Under normal circumstances, my blessing—that was more of a curse—was confined to one night and one night only. Saint Patrick's Day. This year, for the first time since I was eighteen, it slept silently, more than satisfied with the bargain I made. Choosing Liam and love set me free.

Unfortunately, my so-called freedom did not prevent me from being hit on—a downside of practically living at High Tide Tavern. Thankfully, I had a boyfriend who was more than happy to chase away the creeps. If he wasn't around, the team, which had become a second family this past year, was more than happy to step in.

"She's not interested." Liam's deep voice vibrated the little hairs at the back of my neck as he pulled me into his arms. I couldn't see his expression, but I was sure he'd narrowed his eyes into that broody, touch her and I'll knock you out look he gave every man who talked to me.

"Sorry," the man muttered, then turned away, looking for a different soul to seduce.

"It's your fault, you know," Liam said right before dipping his head to kiss my neck.

I pinched my shoulder upward, laughed, then turned to look at him. Even though I picked his outfit, seeing him dressed like a leprechaun—tan trousers, white shirt, green suspenders, and a short scruffy beard that I sprayed orange with temporary dye along with the rest of his hair—made me giggle.

"And how do you figure that?"

"Because you look so damn beautiful." Liam kissed me and just like on the very first night, the world faded away. I would have thought by now that the butterflies and constant need to feel his touch would have faded, but I want him just as much today as I did a year ago. Maybe more.

Liam pulled back and playfully brushed his nose against mine. "Have I told you today how much I love you?"

"Maybe," I whispered, a grin tugging at my lips, "but I wouldn't mind hearing it again." I laced my fingers with his and pulled him toward the back hall. "Upstairs. Where you can show me just how much."

Thank You

I think my biggest thank you for this book goes to my readers. It's been a long time since I published anything, and in this world, unless you're a household name, it's far too easy to fade into nothing. Without releasing a new book every 4-6 months, it's easy to be forgotten, which is why I'm so thankful for my long-term readers who never gave up on me and the new readers who gave me a chance.

Lucky in Love has a fun, no-pressure story. I'd call it a fluff read. Something that just makes you feel happy. Sometimes life is so heavy I just want to read something light. Enter Holly and Liam. I literally JUST realized, as I am typing this, that his name is Liam (no relation to Unexpected). Could I change it? Will I? No. I can't picture this MMC as anyone but LIam.

I'm squirreling. This happens a lot, which is why I sometimes struggle to finish a novel.

I owe a huge thank you to Sam at Bound By Mischief Author Services. She has my back no matter how long it's been since we've talked (because I am horrible at communication) and is ready for everything.

To my mom, who polished this book until it shinned, you rock. I owe you drinks and dinner.

For my husband, who is so supportive but utterly embarrassed that I write... I pray you never read my books. I love you. I love how you know me better than anyone...but stay out of my head.

And to all the people I've probably forgotten because this part of the book is always the hardest, thank you for making it this far with me.

I wouldn't be here without you.

ABOUT THE AUTHOR

I've always wanted to be a writer. I remember my first time really trying to write. It was after I saw Practical Magic and I knew there was more to those characters. Being the creative ten-year-old I was, I managed to write a solid two paragraphs on my mother's dinosaur of a laptop. Fast forward fifteen years, when I was a new stay-at-home mom with no time for friends, let alone a life. I rediscovered my love for reading, which turned into a love of writing. There were A LOT of bad stories in the beginning (those aren't published) but I eventually honed my craft and grew brave enough to publish them in the world.

I'm not a full-time author as of yet. I'm still a mom and a wife and somehow balancing a job along with all the responsibilities tied to adulthood. My writing hours are slim, but man when I dive into a world it's hard to get me out of it.

So far, I've been lucky enough to have readers just as enamored with my characters as I am. It still humbles me that there are readers and bloggers out there willing to take a chance on my stories. So while this is a little bit about me, it's also about you because without your support I wouldn't have a career.

Thank you, from the bottom of my heart, for always believing on me.

Find my socials